Twelve m
Twelve indor
One UNIFORMLY HOT! miniseries.

Don't miss Harlequin Blaze's first 12-book
continuity series, featuring irresistible soldiers
from all branches of the armed forces.

Watch for:

LETTERS FROM HOME by Rhonda Nelson
(Army Rangers—June 2009)

THE SOLDIER by Rhonda Nelson
(Special Forces—July 2009)

STORM WATCH by Jill Shalvis
(National Guard—August 2009)

HER LAST LINE OF DEFENSE by Marie Donovan
(Green Berets—September 2009)

RIPPED! by Jennifer LaBrecque
(Paratrooper—October 2009)

SEALED AND DELIVERED by Jill Monroe
(Navy SEALs—November 2009)

CHRISTMAS MALE by Cara Summers
(Military Police—December 2009)

Uniformly Hot!
The Few. The Proud. The Sexy as Hell.

Blaze

Dear Reader,

I hope that you're enjoying the UNIFORMLY HOT! series as much as I am! These guys are true heroes in every sense of the word. They're tough and honorable and loyal...with a little bit of badass thrown in for good measure.

When active-duty Ranger Levi McPherson—who is currently serving in Iraq—starts getting anonymous sexy love letters from home, he's immediately intrigued and more than a little infatuated.

Then he's given the unexpected opportunity to go home for a few days. And Levi is making it his mission to uncover the identity of his mysterious letter writer—and then indulge in each and every one of her fantasies....

Be sure to look for *The Soldier* next month, when Adam McPherson gets his story. He might have sacrificed part of his leg for God and country, but this soldier still has a lot of offer, whether he realizes it or not.

I love to hear from my readers, so please visit my Web site—www.readRhondaNelson.com—or check out my group blog, www.soapboxqueens.com, with fellow authors and friends Jennifer LaBrecque and Vicki Lewis Thompson. We're always hosting some sort of party in our magical castle.

Happy reading!

Rhonda Nelson

Letters from Home

RHONDA NELSON

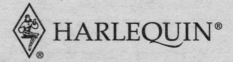

HARLEQUIN®

TORONTO • NEW YORK • LONDON
AMSTERDAM • PARIS • SYDNEY • HAMBURG
STOCKHOLM • ATHENS • TOKYO • MILAN • MADRID
PRAGUE • WARSAW • BUDAPEST • AUCKLAND

Recycling programs
for this product may
not exist in your area.

ISBN-13: 978-0-373-79479-9

LETTERS FROM HOME

Copyright © 2009 by Rhonda Nelson.

www.eHarlequin.com

Printed in U.S.A.

ABOUT THE AUTHOR

A Waldenbooks bestselling author, two-time RITA® Award nominee and *Romantic Times BOOKreviews* Reviewers' Choice nominee, Rhonda Nelson writes hot romantic comedy for Harlequin Blaze. In addition to a writing career she has a husband, two adorable kids, a black Lab and a beautiful bichon frise who dogs her every step. She and her family make their chaotic but happy home in a small town in northern Alabama.

Books by Rhonda Nelson

This book is dedicated with gratitude to every past and present member of our armed forces and to their families who endure in their absence.

I am humbled and so very thankful for your service.

1

March. Baghdad, Iraq

ANOTHER letter. From her.

Levi McPherson felt a current of heat snake through his weary limbs and settle hotly in his loins. A slow smile sliding over his lips, he sank onto the edge of his bed and ignored the various sounds echoing through the concrete barracks. The catcalls, the buzz of laughter, the odd guitar and video-game noises faded into insignificance as he carefully opened the envelope.

Quite frankly, aside from the rare telephone call and e-mail, there was nothing more wonderful to a deployed soldier than a letter from home. Since arriving in Iraq some ten months ago he'd gotten letters from his former unit mates—Lucas "Huck" Finn and Mick Chivers—his parents, his sister, his nieces and nephews, his high-school algebra teacher and, hell, even his boat mechanic.

And he'd appreciated each and every one of them.

But the letters he'd started getting from the Mysterious Ms. X, as Levi had begun to call her, were admittedly the ones he found himself anticipating the most during mail call. Though she never signed her name to any of the letters, but instead ended each steamy missive with a simple "Yours," Levi knew she was a hometown girl because the return address was a post-office box in Bethel Bay, a sleepy little backwater town nestled just north of Hilton Head, South Carolina. *Home,* he thought with a pang of nostalgia, missing the scent of magnolia blossoms and salty sea air. Missing his mother's meat loaf, tag football and sailing.

The last most of all.

Though he wasn't home often enough to justify keeping his boat—a sweet little thirty-three-foot Columbia Boomerang—Levi couldn't quite bring himself to sell it. Being out on the water, hearing the snap of the wind in the sails… Other than being on the front line of a battlefield, it was the only place he'd ever felt grounded. He loved the sea, the expanse and depth, the sheer vastness of it. It was easy to make sense of his own place in the world when he was on the water.

And whoever Ms. X was knew it, too, because she'd mentioned seeing his father taking the *Sabrina* out for a turn around the bay. Levi winced. Damn, he really needed to do something about that name, he thought. Despite the fact that he'd painted over the moniker—that of his ex-fiancée, who'd literally left him at the altar two years ago—the bright-blue letters still bled through. He should have painted them over in black, he thought darkly.

The color would have matched Sabrina's miserable, faithless heart.

Water under the bridge, Levi reminded himself, fishing the letter out of the envelope. It was done. Finished. Over. Better that he find out now that she didn't have the emotional strength to be a military wife. Hell, the first time he'd counted on her to keep the home fires burning, she'd gotten lonely and kept the sheets hot with an old flame. His lips twisted bitterly.

Unfaithfulness was sort of a deal-breaker in his book.

It was all for the best really. He'd been trying to find the kind of love his parents shared and had known deep in his heart that the connection wasn't right with Sabrina. She'd been an ill-planned substitute. Since her, though he'd been left feeling a bit hollow on the inside, Levi had given up on the idea of marriage and family. He'd decided it simply wasn't in his cards.

He heaved a silent sigh and made a mental note to check in with Adam, his little brother, who was also currently serving in Iraq. Not that he necessarily *needed* to check in on him. Only two years younger than him, Adam was a crackerjack soldier, and Levi knew he would always have his back. But old habits died hard and, though it was unreasonable, he couldn't seem to shake the pervading feeling that he needed to protect Adam, that even after all these years, it was still his job.

Shrugging off a bit of unease, Levi unfolded the letter and felt a smile roll over his lips as the familiar feminine writing—neat and a bit loopy—filled the page.

Dear Levi,
I dreamed about you again last night. I dreamed you were home and, more importantly, mine. I dreamed you wanted me, *really* wanted me, that you walked through my front door, our eyes locked and a second later you were on me, taking me hard and fast against the door.

Sweet mercy, was she trying to kill him? Did this woman have any idea how these letters affected him? How therapeutic the ones he wrote back to her were?

You kissed me as though you needed my breath to breathe, you took my breasts into your mouth and suckled the peaks until I almost

came. You slipped your wickedly talented fingers into my panties and I rubbed myself against
you, satisfied…but not, wanting more. Needing
more. I'm hot and muddled now, remembering.

Welcome to the club, sweetheart, he thought,
chuckling darkly. At the moment his balls felt like
they'd been hit with a blow torch.

It was the sort of dream I never wanted to
wake up from, and when I did, I still tingled
with release, imagined I could even still feel you
there, deep inside of me. I ache for you in places
I scarcely recognize, most notably…my heart.

Imagination was an interesting thing, Levi thought,
and in this regard she definitely had the advantage.
She was imagining *him*. Obviously, she knew him.
She'd cited too many little things in previous letters—
including local gossip—not to know both him—and
his brother, for that matter—relatively well.

Meanwhile, his underinformed imagination had
just enough sexy information from her to have him
cocked, locked and ready to rock with a few strokes
of her pen, but he had no face to put with the vision.
Not exactly true. He'd put a face with the vision. An
image of dark-red hair, big brown eyes and a mouth
made for sin suddenly materialized in his mind's

eye. He sucked a breath through his teeth and gave his head a small shake.

Off-limits, he told himself. Don't go there.

It couldn't—*wouldn't*—be her.

He desperately wanted to know Ms. X's identity, but until she slipped up—or he went home to investigate, which in his present situation was out of the question—he was completely at her mercy.

Levi McPherson didn't like being at *anyone's* mercy, but after the Sabrina fiasco, when he'd looked and felt like a damned fool, particularly a woman's.

Furthermore, while the sexy nature of the letters was a stoker, there was something more at work here. He felt a strange sort of connection with his anonymous letter-writer. She *got* him. Truly got him. And that was more of a turn-on than anything she could write.

I know I should probably stop sending you these letters, but I just can't seem to help myself. I'm bleeding my fantasies of you right onto the page—albeit anonymously—and it feels good to finally give voice to my feelings. My desires. I've wanted you…forever, and telling you in detail is the next best thing in the absence of the courage to actually admit who I am. Cowardly, I know, but…

"Levi?"

Levi looked up and saw a couple of his unit mates standing in the doorway. The grave looks on their faces made his heart rate skip into a frantic rhythm and a cold sweat break across his shoulders. And they'd used his given name, not "Remington"—as in Steele—the nickname he'd been given in jump school. Paper crackled in the wretched silence as his fingers involuntarily tightened.

"It's Adam," Will Forrester told him. "Another damned IED."

Miserable roadside bombs, Levi thought as nausea clawed the back of his throat. A punch of panic landed in his gut, momentarily ending his ability to breathe. This had always been a possibility—they were at war, after all, soldiers on the front line of the battlefield. But no amount of mental preparation had readied him for this. He swallowed, dredging deep for the courage he knew he was going to need.

"Where is he?"

"They're bringing him in." Will swallowed. Hard. "He's in bad shape, Levi."

Yeah, well, bad shape was better than dead, Levi thought, relief flooding through him. He'd seen too many damned flag-draped coffins lately, and putting his little brother in one was more than he cared to contemplate.

Hang tight, bro. I'm coming.

2

Dear Levi,
I saw your boat on the bay today and wondered
what it would be like to make love on the water.
You rocking inside of me while the boat rocked
along the waves...

Three months later...

LAST WEEK, WHEN Natalie Rowland's assistant, in a
bout of unusual efficiency, had mistakenly gathered
up her private correspondence along with her art
gallery's promotional mailings and stamped her return address onto what was supposed to have been—
and would forever remain—an anonymous sexy love
letter, then had personally carried it and the rest of
the mail to the post office, Natalie had known a
single blinding moment of panic as she'd belatedly
realized that her private—God help her—*no-longer
anonymous* letter had been posted.

That gut-wrenching, miserable, hyperventilating, nausea-inducing panic paled in comparison with the news she'd just received.

"Levi's c-coming home," she repeated, her voice a strangled croak. A familiar sense of unease made her stomach wobble in warning.

Adam McPherson shifted, barely winced, and tossed the five of clubs onto the discard pile. Though she knew on some level that he had to mourn—and even resent, to some degree—the recent loss of his right leg below the knee, since returning home to his parents' house in Bethel Bay a week ago from The Center for the Intrepid in San Antonio, Texas—the nation's premier facility for amputee and burn victims—he hadn't voiced a single complaint.

She'd catch the occasional broodingly haunted expression, when she knew he was reliving the horror of the incident that had taken part of his leg, but the minute he caught her looking at him, he'd blink away the expression and smile. But that was Adam. A stoic goofball with hidden depths, and one of her oldest and dearest friends.

She'd missed him terribly over the years and had looked forward to his visits home, but admittedly, this was not the sort of occasion she'd been hoping for. His mother had called her as soon as she'd heard the news and had kept her updated until Adam had made it back to town.

Despite the fact that his surgery had gone well and he was healing nicely, recovery would be a long arduous road, but one she had every confidence he would tread with his usual wry humor and determination.

Even if he had to do it with a prosthesis.

His physical therapy was progressing well and, considering the recent advancements in prosthetic technology, he had every intention of returning to active duty as soon as humanly possible. Or so he said and, for his sake and sanity, Natalie certainly hoped so. At the moment Adam was staying with his parents in their beautiful bayside home just a few doors down from her own cottage while recuperating.

Speculation had run rampant during their high-school and college years as to whether their friendship would ever develop into something romantic, but that had never been a possibility. She inwardly smiled.

Probably because she'd been in love with his older brother, Levi, for what felt like most of her life.

Though she'd nursed a crush on Levi during high school—a crush that had started within a few days of the McPhersons' arrival in Bethel Bay after Levi and Adam's father had retired—Natalie could vividly remember the exact moment when she'd fallen in love with him.

It had been another hot summer night at the beach,

just one of many they'd spent gathered around a fire listening to music and hanging out. A few yards down the beach a couple had been arguing and, as time wore on, the fight escalated. Things hit a fever pitch, and the guy backhanded the woman across the face, knocking her to the ground.

Without the slightest hesitation, Levi had raced down the beach and pummeled the hell out of the guy, who at the time had been at least twice his age. *Show some respect, you weak bastard,* he'd said.

And she'd never forgotten it.

Though that had been the defining moment for her, there'd been many more over the years. Levi was the type of guy who never missed an opportunity to do the right thing, even if it was hard. He was always the first to befriend the friendless, to champion the underdog. He was the kind of guy who walked little old ladies across the street, always stopped to help a stranded motorist change a tire and never failed to open a door for a lady. He was a rare combination, a dying breed of man—he was a gentleman and a hero, a beautiful badass who'd made her heart sing.

Levi McPherson. The mere thought of him made something besides her nervous stomach shift and warm in her middle.

And he was coming home.

"Yep," Adam confirmed, much to Natalie's commingled joy and horror. "Today, as a matter of fact." He paused to take a drink of lemonade. From their vantage point on the screened-in porch, they watched a couple of jet skis race around the bay, kicking up a stream of salty spray. "Mom and Dad have gone to Charleston to pick him up. They should be back any minute."

Any minute? Levi? Here? She swallowed, trying not to hurl, a lamentable well-documented side effect of her nerves. Other people broke out in hives or developed a tic. Not her—she puked. Sometimes on people, she thought, remembering that terrible choir incident in fifth grade.

Natalie rearranged the cards in her hand, hoping to disguise the sudden trembling in her fingers, and felt her mouth go bone-dry. Her heart momentarily fainted, then thankfully regained consciousness. She picked up the five, made a run and then discarded the Jack of Hearts.

"Really? I, uh…I didn't think he would get to come home." Small understatement. It had never occurred to her that he'd be home before his tour was up. It hadn't occurred to anyone else, either, she knew. Otherwise the city council—of which she was a part—would have already started planning their welcome-home parade.

"Me, either," Adam said, watching her closely. His eyes twinkled with a humor she didn't altogether trust. "Ordinarily I would have had to come home in a pine box for him to get leave—"

She glared at him in admonishment, not finding the comment the least bit funny. He'd come too damned close to that very scenario. "Adam."

"Sorry," he said, looking a bit repentant. "Bad joke. But I suspect the General pulled some strings. Retired or not, he's still got some friends in high places, and the one in the governor's office, in particular, has called recently."

Natalie had always gotten a kick out of how everyone—including their mother—called Jack McPherson the General instead of Dad. More than likely, though, Adam was right. American troops were stretched thin, so allowing a soldier home— particularly a Ranger like Levi—wasn't the norm, even under these sad circumstances. No doubt their mother's recent cancer scare had played a considerable part in the General flexing his influential muscle to bring Levi back to the States, even temporarily.

She batted a wisp of hair from her eyes, wondering how Levi felt about it. She knew from his letters—the ones he'd written to her via her post-office box—that he was very loyal to his unit and often talked about the brotherhood that existed in the military, particularly in times of crisis. Of course, watching Adam, who was also a part of his unit, leave couldn't have been easy, either. No doubt he was torn between the two.

She cleared her throat, hoping that she sounded marginally nonchalant. "How long will he be home?"

"Just a few days," he said.

Damn. That was still long enough for his mail to be forwarded, provided the evidence of her identity hadn't already arrived. She didn't think so, but…

Honestly, when she'd realized that Lacey, her ordinarily inefficient assistant, had outed her with her return address stamp—damn that stern talking-to she'd given her about being more proactive—Natalie had known an intestine-knotting panic that had almost been enough to bring her to her knees. Little stars had danced behind her lids and the only thing that had prevented her from hurling was the fact that it was physically impossible to hyperventilate *and* throw up simultaneously. Small favors, she reminded herself now, as the panic and nausea made an encore appearance.

Levi. Here. Any minute now.

She still couldn't wrap her mind around it. And, dammit, wouldn't you know she looked like hell? Just her freaking luck. She and her father had been out beachcombing this morning for driftwood—the tool of her trade as a driftwood artist—and had planned to go back this afternoon at low tide. Rather than change clothes for her and Adam's daily Tonk tournament, she'd worn her usual uniform of cut-off denim shorts, a bikini top and a tank. She smothered a miserable whine. She looked like a sea urchin.

Oh, goody.

Though Natalie would love to belong to the don't-worry-about-what-you-can't-change school of thinking, regrettably she'd never been able to embrace the philosophy. That's why she was active on her city council, participated in local charities and made sure to do her part to make the world—or at least her little part of it—a better place. In the grand scheme of things, she knew that Levi finding out that she'd been the one writing the letters wasn't the worst possible thing that could happen to her.

She'd already lived through *that,* thank you, she thought, swallowing tightly as an image of her dear mother rose in her mind's eye.

But the heart wasn't logical, and the part of her that was responsible for pragmatic thoughts was currently trying to keep her breakfast from making an encore appearance,

Would seeing him again under the circumstances be embarrassing? *Oh, dear God, yes.* Had she planned on facing him so soon? Certainly not. In fact, considering that he was deployed for another two months, she'd given herself that long to try and figure out how she was going to handle it. Ordinarily she was more of a take-the-bull-by-the-horns sort of person, but in this instance she just hadn't been able to bear thinking about it. Unfortunately, rather than the two months she'd thought she'd had to formulate a plan, she'd be lucky if she had two minutes.

Sweet God, what was she going to do? Better still, what *could* she do? Provided she could even think of a way to intercept the letter—wishful, lunatic thinking at its best—tampering with the US Mail was a federal offense. While she'd been known to enjoy a prank or two, she'd never slid a toe over the strictly illegal line. Natalie released a small breath.

He was going to find out that she'd written the letters.

Every hot, depraved, *totally uncensored* one of them. It was inevitable, she knew. And then, this strange relationship—the only one she knew she'd ever have with him—would be over. No more letters. No more "talking." No more…anything.

Frankly, she'd long ago given up the hope that Levi would permanently return to Bethel Bay and, after the whole left-at-the-altar-thing Sabrina had put him through she didn't imagine he'd ever settle down.

Least of all with her.

Sad, but true. Oh, he'd always been nice to her. She and Adam had spent enough time together over the years that she'd been around Levi—despite him being a couple of years older—a pretty good bit, but in all that time she'd never detected even the slightest bit of interest in her whatsoever. He was polite. He was kind. He'd crack the occasional joke, but never once had he intimated any sort of interest in her.

Granted, that had all changed with the letters—how many times had he written her back, wanting to know who she was?—but therein lay her present advantage.

Anonymity.

He didn't know who she was. The woman he'd been exchanging correspondence with was the Mysterious Ms. X—his nickname for her made her smile—not Natalie Rowland, hometown girl, little brother's close friend and, most damningly, bridesmaid at his ill-fated wedding.

Honestly, there had been many times in her life when she'd seriously questioned her own judgment— using self-tanning lotion the night before Senior Prom (orange was *not* her color), allowing Adam to talk her into attaching a Wide Load sign onto the back of the somewhat hefty high-school principal's car (detention) and, more recently, trying to make s'mores in the oven rather than the traditional way around a campfire (huge mess). But allowing her father to talk her into agreeing to be one of Sabrina's bridesmaids by far took the Stupid Trophy. Even though she'd never particularly liked Sabrina, as her cousin, it would have been bad form to refuse.

In short, she'd really had no choice.

Despite the fact that she and Sabrina had never been close and she'd had no idea until Adam had told her that Sabrina had been having an affair, Natalie suspected she would always be seen as guilty by association. Frankly, Levi hadn't looked at her the same way since. On the rare but wonderful occasions she'd seen him, he'd always been a bit...distant. Removed.

But better distant and removed than married to Sabrina, Natalie thought, remembering the abject heartache she'd suffered as a result of his proposal to her shallow relation. *Devastated* didn't begin to cover how she'd felt. *Broken, ruined* and *beyond repair* were more accurate descriptions. Though she knew that he'd been humiliated and hurt, Natalie had silently rejoiced when Sabrina had canceled the wedding. And she'd been equally happy when Sabrina had moved to Nashville to pursue her dream of becoming a country-music star last year, Natalie thought, remembering her cousin's horrible warble.

"You okay?" Adam asked. A smile flirted with the corners of his lips. "You're looking a little green."

Adam, damn him, was well-acquainted with her nervous-stomach tendencies, but she'd eat glass before she'd admit that anything was wrong. She blinked innocently. "No, I'm fine."

He studied her for a minute. "I'm glad he's getting a break," he finally remarked, tossing another card down. They'd played every day since Adam had gotten home—Tonk, of course, because it had always been their game of choice. "The time away will help him decompress."

"That bad, eh?" she asked, wincing softly.

Adam swallowed, and one of those rare and fleeting grim looks came over his handsome face. "It's war, sweetheart. It ain't ever pretty."

She knew that. Still... Rather than ask questions she felt sure he didn't want to answer, Natalie hummed under her breath and played another card.

"Of course I expect he'll have his hands full trying to find out who his mystery woman is," he said. Looking decidedly smug, he leaned back in his chair and absently scratched his chest.

Meanwhile Natalie's heart threatened to pound through hers. "Oh?" she croaked. "What mystery woman?" Find her? *Find her?* What in sweet hell was she going to do? *What now, girl genius?*

"That's the question. Levi's been getting letters from a woman from home for months now." He snorted. "Of course the bastard wouldn't let me read them, but I can tell he's pretty damned intrigued by her." He slid her a sly smile. "Interestingly, I noticed that Levi's letters were coming on the same days I'd get one from you."

Oh, shit. Her gaze darted to his and she licked her suddenly dry lips. "You know how the mail is," she said with an airy wave of her hand, cutting the line on his fishing expedition.

Adam considered her long enough to make her want to squirm. "I suppose," he finally remarked. "Still, I do find it a bit odd."

He could find it as odd as he wanted to so long as he didn't *know,* Natalie thought, struggling to bring her heart rate back into a regular rhythm. Geez, Lord, she'd be mortified. Particularly if Adam ever read any of the letters.

They were quite…graphic.

When she'd first decided to start writing Levi, she'd had no idea that she was going to write about her actual dreams and fantasies. She'd just seen a particularly grisly newscast on the war in Iraq, and even though the idea that Levi and Adam might not come home had always hovered in the very back of her mind, for whatever reason, the images, the footage had suddenly made her intensely aware of their mortality.

Her larger-than-life, indomitable friends, badass soldiers…could *die*.

The realization had rattled her to the core and she'd decided then and there that she wouldn't let another sun set without letting them know how she felt. Furthermore, she'd been under the mistaken impression that by writing the letters to Levi, she could somehow exorcise him from her heart. In theory the logic had seemed sound. In execution, it had only made her more intensely aware of how much—how very deeply—she cared for him. And when he'd started writing her back… Well, she'd been done for, hadn't she?

The letters she'd written to Adam had kept him abreast of things happening at home, had been filled with jokes and trivia, but more importantly, with appreciation of their friendship and the sacrifice he was making for their country.

The letters she'd written to Levi—anonymously, of course—had been filled with the deepest desires of her heart. And part of the deepest desires of her heart involved the deepest desire of her flesh.

Hers on his, specifically.

An uneven breath stuttered out of her mouth, and in that instant Levi McPherson strolled around the corner, effectively snatching what little air was left in her lungs. Her body went into a full-on thrill that encompassed every inch of skin from head to toe. She should be used to it by now—it happened every time she saw him—but somehow the sensation caught her off guard.

Dressed simply in camouflage and black combat boots, a lazy smile rolling around his unusually sensual lips, he was the epitome of a true soldier. Courage, confidence and valor were inherent in the way he moved, the shape of his jaw, the noble line of his brow. Broad, competent shoulders, muscled forearms, a lean, tapered waist and long legs rounded out a physique that commanded attention and respect. In short, he was damned fine and her belly quivered in anticipation just looking at him. Her nipples gave a quick tingle and a wave of heat washed over her thighs. In an instant, every wicked, depraved scenario she'd written to him reeled through her mind. *Warm, naked skin. Muscles bunching beneath her fingertips, his hot mouth feasting between her thighs...*

Dimly she watched his parents follow in his wake as he made determined strides toward Adam.

A broad smile lighting his face, Adam grabbed his crutches and started to stand.

"You don't have to get up," Levi told him. She melted inside at the mere sound of his voice.

"The hell I don't," Adam shot back, easily maneuvering himself onto his leg. "I'm not some little old grandma who's going to settle for a one-armed hug." Keeping one crutch tucked up under his shoulder, he nevertheless wrapped both arms hard around his brother and, laughing, squeezed. The boys had always shared a special bond, and never was that more evident than right now.

Natalie stood awkwardly, feeling curiously out of place. The backs of her eyes burned, watching them, and a quick look at Sharon, their mother, confirmed that she was tearing up as well. Even the General appeared choked up as he glanced away and cleared his throat.

"Damn, it's good to see you, little bro," Levi said, drawing back to get a better look at Adam.

"I told you when I left that I'd be fine. You might be older—" He frowned and pretended to peer more closely at Levi's light-brown hair. "—but that doesn't mean that you're the wiser. Is that a gray hair, old man?"

Levi grinned and a bit of relief clung to that smile. "Still a smart-ass I see."

"My sense of humor wasn't in my leg. Y'all have got to stop making a fuss. I'm fine," Adam insisted, sitting back down. And he could insist all he wanted to, but nobody was going to believe him. That perpetual smile he wore didn't quite reach his eyes, and a weariness he couldn't altogether shake hung around his shoulders. "I'll have a brand-new kick-ass leg soon, and if everything goes according to plan, I'll be back with my guys, finishing what we've started."

Natalie noticed Sharon send her husband a furtive look. Obviously his mother didn't approve of that plan. Not that Natalie could blame her, but...

Setting her cards down on the table, Natalie rubbed her suddenly damp hands against her cut-off jeans. "I should be going," she said, not wanting to intrude any more upon their homecoming. She couldn't believe Adam had kept this from her. She wouldn't have come over had she known Levi was coming home today.

Levi's toffee-colored gaze finally swung to hers, inadvertently making her body feel as if it had been plunged into a furnace. A beat slid to three, then a flicker of something that looked impossibly like interest flared in those golden orbs, momentarily making her pulse trip.

But it was what she didn't see that gave her the most relief—he didn't know she was his Mysterious Ms. X.

Or at least, not yet.

"Natalie," he said. To her instant shock and intense delight, he hugged her.

He'd *never* hugged her.

Big, hard and lean, his starched shirt beneath her cheek—it was all she could do to keep from melting all over him. Sweet, wicked sensation bolted through her and she barely suppressed a whimper. In his arms at last, even innocently, was a little dream come true.

And Lord help her how she wanted more.

"It's been a long time," he said, drawing back. Those keen eyes found hers once more, and again she thought she saw a perplexing flash of awareness in his gaze. Her pulse tripped and she felt her heart give a little jump.

Nah, she thought. *It couldn't be.*

She stepped out of his embrace and a wobbly smile faltered over her lips. Wishful thinking, she told herself. Clearly all those letters had fostered a false sense of intimacy. The letters that would stop if he found out she'd written them. Somehow she had to keep him from learning her identity. She had no idea how, of course, but he couldn't discover the truth. It would ruin their so-called relationship and she wasn't willing to give it up. At least, not yet. She wasn't ready.

Truth be told, she would never be ready, but…

"You don't have to go," Adam protested. "We're just going to hang around here." He nodded to Levi's boat, nestled against the dock. "Might even take the *Sabrina* out for a spin after."

Levi's jaw flexed and he shot his little brother an annoyed look. "Second order of business," he said. "Rename the damned boat."

Adam frowned, intrigued. "What's the first order of business?"

"None of yours," Levi answered mysteriously. His gaze jumped back to Natalie's. "But he's right." He jerked his head toward the boat. "The General's had her serviced for me. We're going to take her out this evening if you'd like to come along."

Was he asking because Adam had invited her? Natalie wondered, tempted. "I've got to put in some time at the studio today," she said, hesitating.

As a driftwood artist, she pretty much set her own hours, but she was working on a pair of deer—a doe and a stag—that she was finding particularly en-joyable. She was inexplicably drawn to the stag. The proud angle of his head, the breadth and strength in his shoulders. There was something vaguely familiar about him, but she hadn't been able to put her finger on it yet. She would, she knew, in time. Her art always spoke to her that way and she never failed to learn something about herself during the process.

Levi quirked a light, slanting brow. "Working on something new?"

Adam snorted with wry derision. "You know the answer to that. She's *always* working on something new. That is, when she's not planning the Founders' Day Festival and organizing clean-up crews for the park or directing the Downtown Walking Tours." He pointed to the driftwood pendant around his neck. "She gave me this the day I got home."

Levi studied the shape. "Nice," he said, though it was obvious he didn't have any idea what he was looking at.

"It's the Chinese symbol for courage," Natalie explained, smiling softly.

"Ah," he said, inclining his head. That golden gaze found hers again, causing a little flutter of heat to whisper over the tips of her breasts. "Excellent choice."

"She's brilliant," Adam spoke up. "You should go by her studio, or better still, check out her gallery downtown. Beautiful stuff. Miss Bethel Bay here stays busy." He grinned at her, obviously proud of her accomplishments. "Who would have thought that collecting all that driftwood would turn our little sand rat into an internationally renowned artist?"

"I don't know about that," Natalie said, feeling her cheeks warm under the spotlight of praise. "But it's nice to do what I love to do, have people enjoy it *and* make a living."

Actually, it was more than nice. *Nice* seemed like such an inadequate word when she considered that she was essentially living a dream, albeit a somewhat lonely one. She spent morning and evenings enjoying the beach, the rest of the day in her studio, engrossed in her art. And, thanks to a single sale to an A-list star who made his home in France with his pop-princess girlfriend, people now paid ridiculously large sums of money to own a Rowland original. She'd gone from a gradual success to an overnight sensation. She should be happy—*was* happy—and yet…something was missing. Her gaze drifted to Levi.

She grimly suspected it was the man in front of her.

Seemingly impressed, Levi quirked a brow. "And your dad? Is he still helping you?"

"I couldn't do it without him," Natalie said, rocking back on her heels. Not altogether true, she knew, but her life wouldn't be the same without her father. Since the drowning death of her mother five years ago, John Rowland hadn't let Natalie put so much as a toe in the ocean without him being there, even to gather driftwood along the beach. Another reason going out on the boat with Levi wouldn't be a good idea. Her father would be a wreck with worry.

Molly Rowland had been a strong swimmer, but she'd panicked when caught in a riptide. It seemed so surreal to Natalie, even now. Her mother had been so level-headed. Even-keeled. For months after she'd died, Natalie had sweated through nightmares of her tragic death. She would relive her mother's horrible last moments…the terror, her heart-racing panic, leaden, tired limbs…then this strange acceptance and suffocation. She inwardly shivered, remembering.

Her father had been, in a word, devastated. While Natalie didn't necessarily need his help—she'd managed before—she nonetheless welcomed his presence. Since her mother's death they'd fallen into a comfortable routine. Though she wouldn't say she took care of her father—she had her own place, after all—she nonetheless spent a great deal of time with him.

"What do you say, Nat?" Adam asked. "You want to take a turn around the bay with us?"

Natalie hesitated, torn, but ultimately decided to pass. Levi had just gotten home and, while she knew she was welcome, she thought his mother would probably enjoy having some quality family time.

She gave her head a small shake. "You know, as much as I'd love to, I really can't. Dad and I are combing this afternoon, so…" She looked at Levi. "Maybe another time?"

"Sure," he said. Was it her imagination or was that a fleeting look of disappointment on his face?

She nodded, then bent and gave Adam a kiss on the cheek. She gestured to their game. "I won. You owe me a chick flick." They'd been playing for movies. So far she'd had to watch two horror movies to one chick flick. Now they were even.

Adam chuckled. "I'm not watching *Steel Magnolias* again," he said as she waved goodbye.

Natalie merely smiled, but her insides vibrated with pent-up anxiety and longing as she walked away.

Levi McPherson was home…and his mail was sure to follow. One way or another she had to keep him from getting those letters.

The question, of course, was…how?

3

Dear Levi,
Last night I saw a couple holding hands on the beach and thought of you, my fingers threaded through yours, our lives equally entwined. I could happily hold your hand forever….

"Steel Magnolias?" Levi asked, disturbed that he couldn't take his eyes off Natalie's ass as she walked away. Since his sadistic imagination had cast Natalie as his Ms. X, he knew he hadn't gotten past that inappropriate attraction, but this was too much. Every nerve in his body had sung when he'd laid eyes on her. And touching her. *Damn.* "Do I need to pat her down before she gets to her car?"

"Pat her down for what?"

Levi grinned and waited for their parents to disappear inside the house before responding. "Your balls. You obviously don't have any if you've been watching friggin' *Steel Magnolias* with her," he said, chuckling under his breath. Damn it was good to see him, Levi thought. Physically, his brother looked better than Levi had expected. Mentally, though, he wasn't so sure. There was a strain—a thinness in the skin around Adam's eyes—that alerted him to a deeper-seated problem. Understandable, of course, but he knew his brother would hate the implied weakness.

Adam leaned over and punched him in the arm. "Hey, cut it out. She's been keeping me company."

"I saw that. I hope we didn't interrupt anything." To his annoyance, a bolt of jealousy landed in his gut at the thought.

His brother's gaze sharpened, indicating that he'd gone over the line. "You know it's not like that with me and Natalie. We're friends. That's it." He blew out a breath. "Hell, life would be easier if we *were* into each other. She gets me, you know? She's smart. She's funny. She's beautiful. She's pretty damned close to perfect."

Frankly, Levi couldn't agree more. And she'd looked especially beautiful today. He'd always loved her long, curly hair. A deep red, it slithered thickly over her slim shoulders and perfectly accented those unique dark-brown eyes. A spattering of freckles dusted over her pert nose, emphasizing her elfin features, and her mouth…

Lush, full, raspberry-red and bow-shaped, it was the stuff of fantasies.

His.

Adam sighed heavily and shook his head. "But there's no spark and never has been." He paused thoughtfully and Levi got the distinct impression his brother was thinking about someone who *did* inspire a spark. He let go a breath. "Besides, I have the feeling she's in love with someone else."

Levi's insides twisted uncomfortably. "Really? Who?"

"I couldn't tell you," Adam said, somewhat evasively. "She's never said anything. It's just an impression that I get."

Trying to ignore the sudden pounding in his temples, Levi poured himself a glass of his mother's homemade lemonade and sank onto the porch swing. Because he couldn't think of anything to say that would not result in him looking like a moon-eyed moron, he merely grunted in response.

Honestly, for years now, he'd imagined that at some point Adam and Natalie would tie the knot. They'd always been extremely affectionate with one another, hugging and such, his brother slinging an arm around Natalie's slim shoulders. Granted, Adam had maintained that they were just friends—and if they were in fact "just friends," then they were the exception to the old men-and-women-can't-be-just-friends rule—but Levi had suspected that the relationship would eventually develop into something more. That's why, aside from the Sabrina debacle, he'd kept his distance. He inwardly snorted.

He'd be damned before he'd poach on his brother's turf.

But it had been *damned* hard.

He'd never forget the first time he'd really noticed Natalie, the first time he'd seen her as more than his brother's friend. It had been the summer between their senior year and college. Levi'd been a junior at the Citadel but had come home for a couple of weeks to visit.

Natalie, looking tall and lean and tanned, had been wearing a pair of frayed cut-off shorts and a pink tank top, her bikini strings sticking out from the back. She'd pulled those dark-red, sun-kissed curls up into a messy ponytail and was dancing around the driveway to the tune of Guns N' Roses' "Sweet Child of Mine" as she helped Adam wash his car. Levi had never heard the song again without thinking of her.

She'd been…beautiful.

Fresh, sweet and inherently sexy.

And in that instant, when his dick had gone hard and his heart had given an odd little flutter, he'd realized if he wasn't careful he could fall in love with her. Hell, though Sabrina had been the one to cheat, he had to admit he'd felt a pang of regret for what might have been when he'd seen Natalie at that godforsaken wedding. She'd been a bridesmaid, and had far surpassed the bride.

He grimaced. Hell, that probably should have tipped him off that the idea of marriage was ill-fated. He still didn't know what the hell he'd been thinking. He was career military and, while some guys seemed to know how to make the wife-and-family thing work, Levi wasn't altogether sure he possessed the skill. He'd come home, had panicked because all the guys around him seemed to be moving forward with their lives despite their careers, and he'd unwisely proposed for all the wrong reasons.

He wouldn't make that mistake again.

"Like I said," Adam continued, picking at the bandage around his leg. "I don't know who she's carrying a torch for. But I don't think it's anyone who keeps a permanent address in Bethel Bay." He grimaced and gestured wearily. "Hell, I'm just glad that she's been here this week." His jaw worked and he gestured wearily. "Mom glances at me and cries. The General's trying to keep a stiff upper lip, but can't look me in the eye. Natalie teared up for a minute when she first saw my leg, but it wasn't out of pity—it was because she'd missed me." His determined gaze caught and held Levi's. "You have no idea how nice that was. I don't want to be pitied, Levi. I'm still me. Less of me, yes," he admitted. "But otherwise no different."

As much as he wanted to believe that, Levi didn't. War changed men. You couldn't live through what they lived through and not see things differently. And sustaining an injury like Adam's… Levi swallowed, guilt weighing his shoulders down. He passed a hand over his face. "I'm sorry I wasn't there."

"You weren't supposed to be there, bro. This shit happens. Am I glad that it happened to me? Hell no. Am I occasionally pissed and feel sorry for myself? Hell yes. But this—" He smacked his thigh. "—*this* is not going to define me, you understand? I'm a soldier, by God." He took a pull from his drink. "Nothing's going to change that."

"Mom's worried about you going back," Levi told him. And that was putting it mildly. Their mother wanted Adam to medic out, to come home and find an alternative career. *He's young,* she'd insisted on the drive home. Maybe in years, Levi would admit. But war aged a man in ways that weren't readily seen. Thankfully his father understood that, and, if Adam still wanted to go back to active duty, wouldn't try to stand in his way. Being a soldier was more than a job. It was a mentality, a way of life.

Meanwhile, Levi couldn't help but feel he'd gotten a free pass home. Though the General hadn't admitted to pulling any strings, Levi knew that his father had. Given the state of things in the field right now, there was no way in hell the powers that be would have given him leave.

Was he glad to be home? Oh, hell yes.

Did he regret not being there with his men? Yes to that, too.

Helluva mess, Levi thought, massaging the bridge of his nose. His gaze drifted over his brother's leg. He'd seen too many mangled soldiers, dammit. "How's therapy?" he asked.

"Tough, but it's getting easier."

Thankfully the surgeon who'd performed the surgery had been able to save Adam's knee, which would make his recovery a bit easier, though admittedly there was nothing easy about what his brother was going through. Hopefully when he got his new state-of-the-art prosthesis, he would clear that final hurdle toward putting his life back in order. He'd had multiple fittings and was merely waiting on the device to be ready. Beyond that it would be up to the powers that be whether or not he went back on the front lines.

Levi raised a brow. "Phantom sensation?"

His brother grimaced. "That's a pain in the ass," Adam admitted. "How can something hurt that's not there anymore?"

Levi had heard more than he'd ever wanted to know about phantom sensation, a condition that affected a lot of amputees. Despite the missing limb, amputees often "felt" pain and sensation from their non-existent limb.

"Supposedly it should get better with time," Adam said. "I'm hoping that it goes away altogether once I get my prosthesis." He paused and considered Levi shrewdly. "So what's this first order of business you were talking about?"

Levi chuckled, unsurprised that Adam had gone back to that subject. The boy didn't miss a thing and that was no small part of the reason he was a kick-ass soldier. "I'm going to the post office to set up a temporary box."

A slow, knowing grin slid over Adam's lips. "Afraid you'll miss something important?"

To his horror Levi felt a blush creep up his neck. Him, blushing. A man dubbed Remington in refer-ence to his so-called "balls of steel." He was a damned Ranger, one of the best-trained soldiers on the freaking planet. Rangers *didn't* blush, dammit. "No. I just don't want to miss anything."

Adam laughed. "Correction. You don't want to miss anything from *her.*"

Pathetic, but true, Levi admitted to himself. It was ridiculous how important this woman's letters had become to him. Though he wouldn't have a lot of time at home and needed to spend what little he did have with family, he had every intention of trying to find out who the Mysterious Ms. X really was.

He *needed* to know. *Had* to know.

Was he attracted to the sexy part of her letters? Hell, yeah. They were graphic and erotic and the picture she painted with words made parts of his body react in ways he wouldn't have thought possible. This woman wanted him. Genuinely with-every-cell-in-her-body *wanted* him. He could feel it in each stroke of her pen, read it in every wicked word.

But…it was more than that.

She was funny and open and honest, and there was a familiarity there that he couldn't quite put his finger on, but he knew it existed all the same. A connection, if you will. He couldn't explain his thinking, couldn't make it form anything that remotely resembled common sense, but he knew in his gut that this girl was…special.

For whatever reason, a vision of Natalie and her softly smiling lips suddenly slipped into his mind. God, she'd felt perfect against him. Hugging her had been a mistake, he realized now. Touching her only made him want to touch her more. *Soft, womanly curves.* Perfect breasts and more than a handful of ass. Damn, but the woman had a great ass. Full and heart-shaped and unapologetically feminine. And that scent. A ginger citrus? It was vaguely familiar.

"Tracy Cochran is working at the post office now," Adam told him, a helpful little nugget that immediately made Levi take notice. "She might be able to put a name to a box for you."

Levi's startled gaze darted to his brother's. "That's against the law, isn't it?"

Adam shrugged. "This is a small town and you're a hero. She might be persuaded. That's all I'm sayin'."

Levi didn't know about the hero crap, but he and Tracy had been friends in school. More than friends, actually, he thought, remembering a trip to the beach they'd taken together. It was possible that she might be willing to help him out.

"Word of advice," Adam told Levi, as though he were about to impart something really important. "Don't try to sweet-talk her. If the rumors are true, her girlfriend could kick your ass."

Levi blinked, shock jolting through him. He'd *dated* Tracy Cochran. *"Girlfriend?"*

His brother lifted another unconcerned shoulder. "That's the word on the street."

Levi frowned, still slightly stunned. "You've been busy since you've been home."

Adam smiled at him. "Hell, Levi, this is Bethel Bay. Nothing that's a secret ever stays a secret for long."

Exactly, Levi thought as a slow, purposeful smile slid over his lips. That's precisely what he was betting on.

4

Dear Levi,
Have I ever mentioned how much I want to kiss you? How much I want to taste you? How much I want to tangle my tongue around yours and breathe you in?

WINNIE CUTHBERT—tomboy, fitness nut, baker extraordinaire and longtime best friend—stared at Natalie in unattractive bug-eyed wonder. Icing dripped unnoticed from the pastry bag in her hand, dropping a blob into the middle of a pretty pink rose.

"How could you not tell me about this?" she asked breathlessly. "*You* wrote sexy letters? *To Levi?* I—I—" Smiling, she gestured wordlessly and shook her head. "I'm—"

"Shocked, I know," Natalie supplied, popping another petit four into her mouth. There were times she could scarcely believe it as well.

Winnie's Bakery was the best in town and Winnie

had mastered the almond-icing-to-cake ratio to absolute perfection. If heaven had a flavor, it would taste like one of Winnie's petits fours, Natalie thought, groaning with pleasure. She licked her fingers and enjoyed her friend's stunned reaction. She'd been so busy building her own business and becoming a responsible civic-minded adult that it had been a while since she'd shocked anybody. She'd forgotten how much she liked it.

Furthermore, the fact that she could shock Winnie, who'd been her friend since grade school and who'd been privy to each and every one of her secrets since—with the exception of this one—was quite a coup. She and Winnie had shared lunches, shared crushes, shared heartbreak and shared more phone time than was probably physically healthy, Natalie thought with an inward smile. But she couldn't imagine her life without Winnie.

They had different tastes in music, men and a host of other things, but that would never change the fact that Natalie loved her friend dearly. Theoretically, were Natalie ever to snap and kill someone—there'd been a few times she'd almost launched herself across the board table at a city council meeting—Winnie would be the person she'd call to help her hide the body. It was an unlikely scenario, but the fact remained that she knew Winnie would always have her back.

"So just how sexy were these letters?" Winnie asked, seemingly still gobsmacked. Her periwinkle-blue eyes twinkled with undisguised interest. "R-rated?"

Natalie winced and shook her head.

Winnie's eyes rounded and she leaned forward and lowered her voice despite the fact that the bakery was empty at the moment, a rare occasion. "X? You're telling me you wrote *X-rated* letters to Levi?"

"I told you they were graphic," Natalie reminded her. She slipped behind the counter and helped herself to a glass of peach tea. "And, until Lacey thoughtfully put the return address stamp on my outgoing mail and added the letter to the promo stuff, they were all anonymous." Her cheeks puffed as she expelled a fatalistic breath. "But not anymore."

Winnie set the icing bag aside and dusted her hands on her lavender apron. "Maybe he won't be able to get his mail while he's home."

"He'll make sure that it's forwarded. Adam told me that Levi's stuck on finding out exactly who the letter writer is." She felt a smile roll around her lips. "He's calling me the Mysterious Ms. X."

Winnie's lips twitched. "It has a certain cachet."

"It's a disaster in the making and you know it," Natalie harrumphed. "I've got to get that letter back before he sees it."

"I wouldn't call it a disaster, per se," Winnie countered thoughtfully. Her messy black curls stirred beneath the ceiling fan circling overhead. "More like an opportunity, I would think."

Natalie blinked. "Opportunity? As in opportunity for me to be humiliated beyond words?" Even thinking about the impending moment of truth made a ball of dread the size of a softball form in the pit of her unceasingly churning belly.

"No," she said. "An opportunity for you to stop writing him your fantasies and live them out in the flesh."

Abruptly Natalie pushed away from the counter, grabbing Winnie's toned arm in the process to propel her toward the door. "Okay, let's go."

"Go where?"

"To rehab. You've obviously started smoking crack."

Winnie chuckled and dug in her heels. "Natalie, come on. You had to know when you started writing him the letters that he might discover your identity."

Natalie rolled her eyes and shot her friend an incredulous look. "You know damn well I don't ever think that far ahead." She rubbed her temples. "I just—I just started writing him and he kept writing me back and, and…" *It was the closest thing to a relationship she'd ever had or would have with him.*

And that was it, Natalie realized. Being found out would be mortifying as hell, but it was knowing that this unique connection would soon be broken that upset her the most. She'd rather have this fantasy relationship with him than nothing at all.

It was official. She was pathetic.

Winnie made a sympathetic moue of regret. "And you don't want it to end?"

"Exactly." She swallowed, trying to make sense of her own feelings. "When he finds out who I am, it's over, you know? No more letters. No more sharing fantasies or dreams or…anything." She'd learned so much about him over the past few months, things she'd never imagined that he would confide in her. "It'll be awkward and weird and things will never be the same."

"Does Adam know?"

Natalie chuckled darkly. "Er…no. I confide a lot in Adam, but telling him that his brother makes me find new and ingenious uses for my massaging showerhead isn't one of them."

"Natalie!"

Smiling, Natalie shrugged with unrepentant humor. "I'm just sayin'." She paused. "You still haven't been by to see him?"

Her friend winced and a flash of pain and regret darkened her blue gaze. "I—I can't yet. I will," she insisted.

Winnie had carried a torch for Adam for almost as long as Natalie had for Levi. To date, though they'd been friends and competitors and were constantly one-upping each other when it came to sports, a fact that had bordered on the obsessive and provided ample entertainment, Adam had never shown any romantic interest in Winnie. Like Natalie, Winnie had dated a few guys off and on throughout high school and college, but had never settled in for what one would call a long and meaningful relationship.

Probably because Adam held a key ingredient to any successful pairing—Winnie's heart. Those McPherson boys had a way of unwittingly rendering every other guy insignificant. If the rumors were true, she'd been nicknamed Just-Say-No-Natalie because she routinely refused anything remotely resembling a date. What was the point, really? She'd tried to move on in college, had even given her virginity away in the process, and for what? In the end, there was only one guy for her. Her gaze slid to her friend.

She grimly suspected the same was true for Winnie.

Natalie smiled softly. "You need to go see him."

A wobbly grin formed on Winnie's lips. "I know that, Natalie. I'm just not so sure that I won't cry. And he doesn't need that, you know? He'd resent me for it."

Adam definitely didn't want to be pitied. Natalie had done all of her crying for his injury before he got back into Bethel Bay, and the only tears she'd shown him since were tears of joy for his homecoming. Winnie was right. Adam was damned intuitive and wouldn't appreciate her pity. Especially from Winnie, who'd always challenged him.

But he would appreciate her petits fours.

"Take him a box of your goodies," she suggested. "If you think you're going to cry, then tell him you've got to make another delivery."

"I might."

She took her by the shoulders. *"Do."*

"How do you think he's going to feel about the letters you've written to Levi?"

Natalie made a moue of regret. "You mean other than ragging me mercilessly about it for the rest of our natural lives? He'll be fine. Actually…I think he already suspects."

"Really? What makes you think that?"

She grimaced. "Because I am a moron and he's rather observant."

Winnie shook her head. "Er…afraid I'm not following."

"He noticed that my letters to him and the Mysterious Ms. X's letters to Levi were arriving on the same day."

Winnie's eyes rounded in disbelief. "You mean you mailed them at the same time?"

"I was being efficient," Natalie defended, nevertheless disgusted with herself. "We both know I'm incapable of being otherwise." It was no small part of the reason she was such a good council member.

She was one of those rare people who were neither right nor left brained. She was equally strong on both lobes, which made her a bit of an oddball when it came to being an artist. Many artistic types were scatterbrained and disorganized. Not her. Even her studio was methodically categorized.

She was sort of like Winnie, Natalie thought. Her friend's tomboy nature and penchant for sports— softball and running, in particular—seemed completely at odds with the fact that she owned a bakery and was able to make little bits of edible heaven. Winnie was equally happy being covered with dirt or covered in icing. It was part of her charm, Natalie thought, glancing around the bakery, admiring her friend's handiwork.

The inside of the bakery itself looked good enough to eat. Varying shades of lavender accented with silver filigree decorated the walls, and black and white tiles lay in a harlequin pattern on the floor. Fresh flowers and whimsical accessories rounded out the quirky decor. Huge picture windows framed Bethel Bay proper, and Natalie's heart inexplicably swelled with pride as she looked out onto the quaint cobblestoned streets.

Hanging baskets bursting with colorful blooms hung from black wrought-iron lampposts, and the sidewalks were full of barrel planters. Begonias and marigolds marched in little regimented rows along flower beds at every street corner, and the scent of the ocean wafted in on the constant breeze. Bethel Bay was an old town and had managed to grow with the times without sacrificing its heritage.

Thanks to a city council—one that Natalie was proud to be part of—dedicated to preserving their little burg, prime real estate still remained in the downtown area rather than being spread out along the new highway. Various tax incentives to encourage new businesses to open in the older renovated buildings had ensured that the "little man" wasn't being squeezed out by the big box and chain stores and the result was a wonderful atmosphere for residents and vacationers alike. Slate-shingled roofs, stained glass and copper fixtures were the prominent architectural features, creating a warm, picturesque mood along the square.

Natalie loved her little town. She'd grown up walking these streets—getting salt water taffy from the local candy store, buying her school supplies at the five-and-dime, her prom dress from Waterstone's Formals on the corner. She'd spent her summers on the beach, combing for driftwood, building bonfires and having clambakes. She smiled. She'd spent her winters doing much of the same. This little town had shaped her life, had influenced her art. She'd built her business here and no one was more proud of her than her local "family."

Home, Natalie thought. Just another reason to add to a list of many for why things could never work out between her and Levi. She was invested here. Her father, her business, her very way of life.

He was not.

Levi McPherson was a soldier first and foremost and she couldn't picture him ever returning to Bethel Bay on a permanent basis. And since she would never leave...well, having the "letter relationship" was the only one that would have worked.

And the minute his forwarded mail caught up to him it would be over. She let go a sigh that felt dredged up from the very bottom of her heartsick soul.

"So what are you going to do?" Winnie asked.

"What any right-thinking, successful, mature woman of twenty-seven would do, of course," she said matter-of-factly.

"Tell him? Get the jump on him? Take the bull by the horns, so to speak?"

Natalie looked at her friend as though she'd lost her mind, then snagged another petit four for the road and headed toward the door. She needed to drop by the studio. "Hell, no." She smiled over her shoulder. "I'm going to avoid him. At least until I can find a way to get my hands on that letter before he does."

As a matter of fact, the letter getting routed through

Bethel Bay might actually give her the advantage she needed. A minuscule hope, but she'd take it where she could get it.

"Levi McPherson, as I live and breathe."

"Hey, Tracy," Levi said, leaning casually against the counter. He'd waited for a lull at the post office, but knew it wouldn't last. He needed to act fast, but imagined he'd have to go through the requisite chit-chat first. "How's it going?"

Short and a little heavier than he remembered, Tracy beamed at him. "Great. God, it's good to see you." A shadow moved over her face. "Sorry to hear about Adam, though. I hope he's doing okay."

Levi nodded, accepting her sympathy. "Thanks. But you know Adam. He'll be fine. We're just thankful that it wasn't any worse." Understatement of the year. They were eternally thankful he'd only lost part of his leg, rather than his life. Now the only thing that remained to be seen was whether or not he could reclaim his former way of life.

She tossed a box into the bin behind her. "You on leave?"

"Just for a few days. I've had my mail forwarded to my parents' while I'm home, but wondered if you wouldn't mind holding it for me here instead? I'll come by regularly."

She gave him an odd look. "You don't want a box?"

Slightly embarrassed, Levi shook his head. "It would be sort of a waste."

She nodded knowingly. "You're right. I don't mind holding it for you at all. They're usually finished sorting by nine every morning. I'll keep any mail up here for you."

"Thanks. I appreciate it." He hesitated, looked away then found her gaze once more. "Look, this is a bit awkward, but I wondered if you could do me a favor?"

"I will if I can. What do you need?"

He smiled and passed a hand over his face. "I need to know who owns box 270."

Undisguised interest sparked in her eyes, but she ultimately frowned and shook her head. "Sorry, Levi. I can't tell you that. It's illegal."

Damn, he thought as disappointment knifed through him. He'd figured as much, but it was worth a try. He pushed away from the counter and smiled at her. "No problem. I knew it was a long shot."

A sly grin slid over her lips. "Any particular reason you want to know who owns box 270?"

"Idle curiosity, that's all."

She hummed under her breath, clearly not convinced.

Levi grinned at her and, shaking his head, made his way to the door. "Thanks, Tracy. I'll see you in the morning."

"Hey, Levi?"

He turned.

"I can tell you that the owner of box 270 typically checks mail in the afternoon, around fourish, I think," she added speculatively.

Hot damn. It was a start. He smiled gratefully and nodded. "Then I'll see you tomorrow afternoon instead. And…thanks."

"Anytime."

Feeling marginally better now that a plan was in place, Levi pushed out onto the sidewalk and inhaled the unmistakable scent of home. Salty air and magnolias, pine mulch and seafood. The sun was sinking midway through the sky, casting shadows along the bricked sidewalk. He looked one way and then the other, trying to choose his path, when he noticed Natalie's sign—wrought-iron and suspended from a huge piece of driftwood—hanging from her storefront just a few doors down.

Path chosen, he thought as his feet instantly took the direction that would lead him to her door. A bell tinkled overhead, heralding his presence and, though he could hear voices in the back, no one came forward. Just as well, because he wanted to take an uninterrupted look around.

He whistled low, impressed. Life-sized animals in various poses stood on pedestals stationed around the room. Horses—a mare and her colt. Dolphins, otters, cats and dogs. Even a wolf. Aside from being haunt-ingly beautiful, each piece had a…soul, for lack of a better explanation. It was as though she'd seen every one of these animals and made their driftwood counterpart.

Utterly amazing.

In addition to the larger pieces, shelves were full of earrings, pendants, bowls, and wind-chimes fash-ioned from sea glass. He carefully picked up a drift-wood rabbit, inspecting how she'd put it together. Each piece of wood fitted perfectly, creating seamless lines for the animal's limbs.

Honestly, he'd known she was talented, had even admired the heart she'd fashioned for his parents for their fortieth wedding anniversary, but he'd had no idea, no real appreciation for the scope of her talent. No wonder she—

"Dad, this is crazy—you have to go," Natalie said, emerging from the back room. "Uncle Milton needs your help. It's a week, not the end of the world. I've got plenty here to keep me busy. I can wait until you get home to go combing."

John Rowland ambled into view. "I know you can, girl. But we both know you won't. Stubborn," he muttered. "Just like your mother."

Unwilling to let the conversation continue without making his presence known, Levi cleared his throat.

Natalie's dark-brown eyes quickly found his, and

the impact of those coffee-colored orbs made his legs go a bit weak. Desire, hot and fierce, bolted through him, sending a current of heat straight to his loins.

Little brother's best friend, he reminded himself. *Inappropriate. Out of bounds.* Since the Sabrina incident, the only kind of woman he dallied with was the temporary kind, and Natalie Rowland—hot and tempting as she might be—definitely wasn't the type for the fleeting affair he typically enjoyed. And even those were few and far between.

Furthermore, he preferred having all of his body parts accounted for and in working order—specifically his balls—and knew that his brother, who was well acquainted with his sporadic dating habits, would castrate him in a heartbeat for messing around with his friend. Besides, he had things to do.

Like putting a real name to the Mysterious Ms. X.

Natalie's gaze dropped to his mouth, making his lips tingle in response. His gut constricted and his balls hardened in his briefs.

Bad, bad idea.

Interestingly, he could have sworn that he saw the same flash of awareness mirrored in her gaze as well. He frowned slightly, studying her.

"Levi," she said, a little too cheerfully. "What brings you here?"

"You, of course. I wanted to see what you've been

up to." He nodded at the mare and colt. "Impressive stuff. It's beautiful."

She wandered over, crossed her arms over her chest, inadvertently pushing her breasts tighter against her shirt, and sighed. "Thank you," she murmured softly, seemingly embarrassed by his praise. For reasons that escaped his immediate understanding, he found this utterly adorable.

"How long does it take you to do something like this?"

She shrugged. "It depends. If all the pieces are there, I've been known to work without sleep for a couple of days to finish something."

"She pushes herself too hard," her father piped up.

"Dad," she said warningly.

"That's another reason I'm not going to Milton's."

Intrigued, Levi arched a questioning brow.

Natalie released an exasperated sigh and leaned closer to him. He caught her scent and felt another inappropriate surge of lust. "Uncle Milton has to have surgery on his foot. He's not going to be able to get around for a week or so, and he's asked Dad to come up and stay with him." She jerked her head in her father's direction and lowered her voice. "Hardhead over there doesn't want to go."

"Because he doesn't want to leave you?"

A light blush tinged her cheeks and she shrugged, seemingly embarrassed. "Because he doesn't want me going to the beach alone. Not since Mom—"

Ah, Levi thought, as understanding dawned. He remembered when Natalie's mom had drowned. Terrible stuff. In a seaside community there were accidents every year, but Molly Rowland was a born-and-bred Bethel Bay girl who'd been an Olympic hopeful on her college swim team. Her death had rattled the community to its core and had left Natalie and her father devastated.

Natalie cleared her throat and toed the carpet absently with her sandal. "Anyway, it's ridiculous. I'm an adult. I know how to swim, and it's not like I'm going into the ocean anyway, you know? Just along the water's edge."

He could see her point, but also understood John's anxiety, irrational as it might be. He watched her father from across the store, noted the worry lines around his drawn mouth, the crease of concern written across his forehead.

"I'll go with you," Levi said, surprising himself.

Natalie blinked, startled. "What?"

"I'll go combing with you so that you're not alone." He gestured toward her father. "Do you think that would work for John?"

A flash of unreadable emotion—fear, maybe?— lit her gaze, but she blinked it away before he could form a proper opinion. "You don't have to do that, Levi," she said, her voice strangely high-pitched and shaky. "You need to spend time with your family."

If he didn't know any better he'd think she was purposely trying to avoid him, which didn't make any sense. Natalie had always seemed comfortable in his company. Had something changed? he wondered, studying her closely.

"I'll have plenty of time with my family," he said, suddenly determined to help her whether she wanted him to or not. Irrational, he knew, but he couldn't seem to help himself. He wanted to be with her. Needed to, which didn't make any sense. "I love to walk along the beach. I've missed the ocean." He passed a hand over his face. "I've missed home."

"Really?" She sounded annoyingly surprised.

His gaze swung to hers. "Yeah, I love Bethel Bay." He rocked back on his heels and chuckled softly. "Could I live here permanently? No. I'd go stir-crazy, but it'll always be home."

And it was the truth. That was part of the draw of the military life. He'd loved being an army brat as a kid growing up, and enjoyed the lifestyle even more as an adult. He'd traveled all over the world, had been stationed in all four corners of the globe at one point or another, and had loved every minute of it. He thrived on learning about new cultures and, hell…just breathing different air. Though he knew he would eventually retire here—much like his father had and Adam planned to do—that was years from now. And even after he retired, he'd still want to travel.

He paused to look at her. "What about you? Ever thought about moving away from here? Living somewhere else?"

She grinned, almost sadly, which seemed very odd to him, and she let go a small, almost imperceptible sigh. "Not once."

Unsure of what to make of her, Levi merely smiled. "You don't know what you're missing."

That coffee-colored gaze tangled with his, making his chest grow inexplicably tight, and an unmistakable arc of awareness passed between them. "The same could be said for you."

"Where's the phone book?" John called out, rifling through drawers behind the counter, thankfully interrupting the strange moment. "Surely there's some sort of home care Milton could use. I don't have time to…"

Natalie heaved another exasperated breath and shot Levi a look. "You're sure you don't mind?"

"I wouldn't have offered if I did."

As a matter of fact, he was looking forward to it. More than he should, if he were completely honest with himself. He didn't know what exactly had prompted the offer, but it felt…right. It felt strangely *necessary*. Levi inwardly grimaced as another thought struck.

No doubt Adam would be only too happy to tell him how wrong it was.

5

Dear Levi,
My belly goes all hot and muddled when I think about what it would be like to feel my naked skin against yours....

"I THOUGHT you said you were going to avoid him until you could figure out some way to intercept that letter," Winnie said. "What happened?"

Wedging the phone in between her ear and her shoulder, Natalie reached for the remote control and settled into the corner of her couch. Geraldine, her unusually small tabby cat, curled into her side, purring contentedly. "That was the plan," Natalie told her, blowing out a breath. "But Dad is leaving for Uncle Milton's in the morning for a week and he originally didn't want to go because he didn't want me going to the beach alone."

Winnie made a wincing noise. "Natalie, I understand why he feels that way, but you've got to put a stop to this. You can go combing by yourself. You did it for years before your mom's accident. Has he forgotten that?"

"He's chosen to forget, I think." And her friend was right. Her father's obsessive fear over her and the ocean, while understandable, was becoming a problem.

In the beginning she'd indulged her father because it had given them something to do together, something important that helped take their minds off what they had lost. Her father was "protecting" her. She got that. But, as Winnie had pointed out, when his obsession with her safety interfered to this extent...it wasn't healthy.

For either of them.

"You know what he needs, don't you?"

Natalie idly flipped channels, looking for something interesting to watch. "No, what?"

"A girlfriend."

Ha. Winnie didn't have to tell her that. "You know I've tried to get him to consider dating again. Eloise Dawson is crazy about him, but he won't give her the time of day. She's cooked meals for him and taken them by his house, she's helped him with his roses." She snorted indelicately. "She's all but spread herself out like dinner on the ground and he won't have any part of it." She paused and poked her tongue into the side of her cheek. "And here's the kicker. I think he actually likes her."

"He's that devoted to your mother's memory?"

"Yeah, he is," Natalie said softly. "It's sweet and selfless and noble. But it's also stupid. She wouldn't have wanted this. She would have wanted him to be happy."

She picked at a loose thread on her Pepe Le Pew pajama bottoms and her gaze slid to the black-and-white picture of her parents on their wedding day that she kept on her mantel. Her heart gave a little squeeze. They'd been so in love. She wanted that, Natalie thought wistfully. She wanted a man to look at her the way her father was looking at her mother in that picture. She wanted to be worshipped and adored, flaws, foibles and all.

Specifically, she wanted Levi to look at her that way.

A melancholy smile twisted her lips. And while the Almighty was handing out miracles, she'd also like a unicorn if it wasn't too much trouble. And to be a mermaid on the weekend.

"I know you miss her." Winnie's gentle words brought her back to the moment.

"I do." More than she could have ever imagined. "And he does, too. Which is why it's so hard for me to tell Dad that I don't need him to go to the beach with me anymore. Right now it's his purpose in life, you know? How am I supposed to take that away from him?"

"It's called tough love, sweetie. He needs to shift his attention to something else."

She agreed. But having the nerve to tell him that was not easy. Maybe staying with Uncle Milton for a little while would be good for him. A little distance might give her father some much-needed perspective.

And God knows she could use some of her own.

Levi McPherson. Beachcombing. With her.

It was one of her favorite dreams and worst nightmares all rolled into one. As Winnie helpfully pointed out, how was she supposed to avoid him if he took over for her father? And there was no telling him to forget about it once her father left. Levi was many things—fearless, gorgeous, wonderful, honorable, had integrity in spades, a fabulous sense of humor and a body that she'd like to make her personal playground for a little while, preferably forever. But above all else, he was a man of his word and he'd promised her father that he wouldn't let her go out alone.

In the event that she couldn't intercept that letter, he would find out she'd been sending him those sexy missives…and she'd still have to keep company with him.

She'd be mortified.

In the meantime she had to figure out a way to get that letter back before it landed in Levi's hot little hands. Frankly, she didn't have any idea how this would even be possible.

In the first place, tampering with the mail was against federal law. In the second place, even if she could get a little inside help at their local post office—Tracy Cochran, maybe?—it would involve bringing another person into her confidence. She hadn't even summoned the nerve to tell her best friend until this morning. How in the hell could she confide in Tracy? Furthermore, though Natalie liked the woman well enough, asking Tracy to keep a secret was like asking a Baptist preacher not to have an altar call at a tent revival—impossible.

Unfortunately she didn't see that she had any other choice and planned to ask for Tracy's help first thing in the morning before she and Levi made their way down to the shore.

Honestly, when she'd walked out of the back room and seen him standing in her gallery this afternoon, she couldn't have been more stunned. Though she knew Adam had suggested that Levi come by, she'd never really imagined that he would. Funny, that. She'd been so busy imagining all sorts of other things with him— sex, mainly—and yet she'd never imagined him just turning up in her shop. Today, when he'd been looking at her, she could have sworn that she saw another little sparkle of interest in those intense pale brown eyes. There'd been a hint of something slightly wicked in the curve of his smile, something downright sexual about the way he'd been staring at her mouth.

And then when he'd volunteered to go to the beach with her…

She'd gone from merely stunned to dumbstruck. And the more she'd tried to convince him that he didn't have to put himself out, the more determined he'd become. Honestly, if she didn't know any better she'd swear he'd been flirting with her.

Which was crazy…wasn't it?

She cocked her head, thoughtfully considering the idea. He'd never been interested in her before and she was still the same old Natalie she'd always been. Passably attractive, but no real looker. She wouldn't make a dog point, but knew she wouldn't win any beauty contests either. She had too many freckles on a too-small nose and too much junk in the trunk to be anything other than average. Which, in the grand scheme of things, was fine.

At any rate, she had to be reading things wrong and wouldn't allow herself even to consider any-thing else. It was too risky to hope for more. She'd been pining away for Levi for years—to the point that she'd stopped dating altogether—and had finally, in a weird sort of way, come to terms with the situation through their letters. She'd confessed her feelings, she'd shared every depraved thought. She might not have bared her identity, but she'd bared her soul and, in return, had been given a peek at his.

It *had* to be enough.

Because, at the end of the day, a romance between them would be a dead end. He'd never stay in Bethel Bay—had said so himself today, she remembered sadly—and she couldn't see herself leaving, even for him. How could she leave her dad? Her family and friends? Her responsibilities and her town? She couldn't wrap her head around it. Couldn't imagine a life, even with Levi, away from Bethel Bay. Did she ever long to travel? To see the world? Yes. She'd love to wander foreign shores, to visit the Louvre, to admire the ancient ruins of Greece. But to be gone indefinitely? No. Bethel Bay was home. It would always be home.

"So your dad heads to your uncle's in the morning?"

Natalie sighed. "He does."

"And Levi's coming over?"

"I offered to pick him up, but he's just going to walk down and we'll leave from here."

"He hasn't seen your place, has he?"

"Not in its finished form. It was still under construction the last time he was home."

Winnie gave a little sigh. "I love your house."

A chuckle bubbled up Natalie's throat. "I do, too."

"When I can finally afford to build, I'm going to blatantly steal the whole shebang. The double veranda, the Bahama shutters, even the cupola."

Smiling, Natalie shook her head. Her friend had said as much before. "So long as you don't build next door, I don't care."

"I can't build next door. Your father won't sell the lot."

Natalie knew that and couldn't imagine why not. He could put a tidy little chunk of change into his retirement fund if he'd let it go, but for whatever reason, John insisted that he'd just hang on to the property.

As for her house, she loved it, too. It had simple lines with a nod to Colonial and standard beach-cottage architecture. She'd opted for tall ceilings, lots of hardwood, molding and beadboard and enjoyed the open layout. Her master suite and studio were downstairs, two bedrooms and a bath on the second floor. Nothing complicated, but the building as a whole had turned out to be quite charming, if she did say so herself.

"I still think you need to abandon this whole get-the-letter-back approach," Winnie said. "Honestly, I think it's a waste of your time—what little of it you have with him—and it's a futile effort. It's not going to work."

"Winnie—"

"No, listen," her friend insisted. "You told me the reason that you started writing the letters was because you were afraid he wouldn't come back."

Natalie swallowed. She still was. She couldn't

watch the news or listen to the radio or log onto the Internet without being reminded of the very real danger Levi, Adam and every other member of the American military forces in Iraq faced.

"Is this really how you want to spend this time with him, Natalie? Trying to avoid him? Spinning your wheels to come up with a way to retrieve that damned letter? Did it ever occur to you that all of this has happened for a reason—that Lacey was *supposed* to smack that return-address stamp on that letter? That he's here now, and you've got a chance to tell him how you feel? To *show* him how you feel? Don't settle for that letter relationship, sweetheart." Her voice softened. "You deserve better and so does he. You've been in love with the boy for as long as I can remember. *Go for it.*"

Would that she had the courage, Natalie thought, swayed by Winnie's reasoning. What if her friend was right? What if this was her only chance? Her only shot? "Winnie, I don't know that I—"

"Just think about it," her friend insisted.

Natalie swallowed. Given the argument Winnie had just presented, it would be damned hard to think about anything else.

"STRANGE, isn't it?"

Levi blinked, then turned and looked at his brother. They'd taken the boat out—damn, it had been great to be back on the water: the smell of the sea, the wind in the sails—then had come home and settled in on the screened-in porch once again. The buzz of the television droned through the open window and the scent of his mother's apple dumplings wafted out on the night breeze.

"What?" he asked.

"Being home. It's too—"

"Quiet," Levi finished, chuckling under his breath. He knew exactly what Adam meant. He'd gotten used to the sights and sounds of war, of comrades and gunfire, of heavy artillery and shouting. He gazed out over the bay, watched the wind move through the willow trees and felt curiously disconnected from it all. And for his peace of mind, he knew he had to stay that way. He couldn't afford to want this. It wasn't part of his plan, and it damned sure wasn't in his future. He had a tour of duty to finish, a country to serve and protect, and guys back in Iraq who were waiting on him to help them finish their mission.

This, beautiful as it was, could only be temporary.

And though occasionally he longed for something…more, Levi couldn't remember a time when he didn't want to be a soldier. While other boys had been playing with toy cars, he'd been building dirt forts for his plastic army men. He'd loved growing up on army bases, watching the men in their uniforms, the confidence and purpose in their steps. He'd admired his father, who'd instilled a love of his country and its history into his blood.

Being a soldier…it was more than what he did. It was who he was.

And it was damned hard to date, much less find someone he might want to attach himself to permanently when he was in the middle of a war.

Furthermore, the only time he'd given it a shot, the whole damned thing had blown up in his face and made him a laughingstock. His gaze slid to his boat. *So help me God, I'm painting over that name tomorrow,* Levi thought. After he went beachcombing with Natalie, of course. That prospect brought a smile to his lips.

"What are you grinning about?" Adam asked suspiciously.

Levi scowled as a flash of heat hit his cheeks. "Nothing."

"Doesn't look like nothing, Remington," Adam said, using his Ranger nickname.

During jump school, Levi had taken one particularly daring jump, and Mick Chivers, one of his best friends, who had recently gotten married and become a father, had made the remark that he must have "balls of steel." That had led to Remington Steele jokes and the nickname, which was eventually shortened to just Remington.

"Looks like you're thinking about her again. Ms. X, right? Was Tracy helpful today?"

"Not particularly," Levi told him.

And he hadn't been thinking about Ms. X—he'd been thinking about Natalie, but it was probably better if he didn't share that little tidbit with Adam. In fact, since seeing her this afternoon he'd done little else *but* think about Natalie.

Not good.

And for the life of him, he didn't understand it. Yes, he'd always had a thing for her, one that he'd admittedly, with increasing difficulty, managed to keep under control. Evidently that ability had gone by the wayside. Otherwise he wouldn't have blurted out that offer to go beachcombing with her while her father was away.

Levi had tried to tell himself that he'd made the suggestion out of ordinary kindness, that it was the "nice" thing to do…but he knew better. He'd offered because he wanted to spend some time with her. Because he'd seen a brief but memorable glimpse of haunted longing in her own eyes this afternoon when he'd stopped by. It had been a bit of a shock, but one he had to admit he found rather gratifying.

And because he was a glutton for punishment and an opportunistic bastard, he had every intention of taking advantage of the situation. Despite every warning bell going off in his head, he wanted her.

Still.

Adam blew out a breath. "Well, damn. I was hoping she'd share a little information with you. I didn't expect her to tell you who owned that post-office box, but I was hoping she'd point you in the right direction. Maybe drop a hint."

"She did say that the owner of the box checked mail around four."

Adam gazed at him thoughtfully. "Well, that's a start. And it shouldn't interfere with going to the beach with Natalie. She typically finishes up at the gallery around that time, then goes down to the shore."

In the process of lifting his drink to his lips, Levi paused. "You're awfully familiar with her schedule for someone who's just a friend."

"That's beginning to wear thin, brother," Adam said, staring at him in a way that was too close for comfort. "If I didn't know any better I'd say you were sounding a little jealous."

Damn. "Then it's a good thing you know better."

Adam merely smiled then looked away. "I know her damned schedule because she's been coming by in between working at the gallery, working in her studio, beachcombing, going to her city council meetings, this meeting and that meeting." He chuckled softly. "She's got a finger in every friggin' pie in Bethel Bay."

Levi had gathered that from various things Adam had already mentioned. Natalie had more than mere "ties" to the community. She was shackled to it. Out of love, he knew, but it nevertheless made him uncomfortable. The thought just reinforced his point that getting involved with her would be a bad idea. She was invested here. He was invested in his career. It was a no-win situation that had disaster written all over it.

Pity it didn't make him want her any less.

"Anyway," Adam continued, "we've played Tonk and hung out. It's been nice. Nat's easy company. She doesn't ask a lot of questions I don't want to answer, you know? She's just…Natalie."

For someone who was so outgoing, Adam was intensely private, played his cards close to his vest and kept a tight circle of friends. No doubt Natalie understood that and treated him accordingly. She wouldn't ask him a lot of prying questions, she'd just be there, which was, no doubt, exactly what his brother needed at the moment.

"You know the minute John leaves she's going to try and shake you, right?" Adam asked.

Levi quirked a brow. "Why would she do that?"

"Because she's perfectly capable of going to the beach alone and will resent having a babysitter."

"I'm not a babysitter. I simply stepped in so her father would back off and go to his brother's."

"Preachin' to the choir. But I know her. She's stubborn."

"I promised her father that I'd go with her." And he would. The end.

"What time are you supposed to meet her in the morning?"

"Eight."

"I'd get there at seven-thirty."

Levi frowned. "You really think she'll leave without me?" That seemed a little out of character, but admittedly, Adam knew Natalie better than he did.

Adam merely shrugged. "It wouldn't surprise me. So, what are you going to do? Start staking out the post office? Watch who's going in and out around four?"

"Something like that."

"And if it doesn't work?"

"I'll cross that bridge when I come to it. Maybe see if Louis will help me out."

Louis Johnson had been their mail carrier for years and had always had a soft spot for their mother, who never failed to tuck a little something extra into the box for him on holidays. He might not be willing to find out for Levi, but Levi knew it'd be damned hard for Louis to tell his mother no.

Adam whistled low. "You're going to enlist Mom's help? *Wow*."

Naturally, he'd rather not. Telling his mother about the sexy letters wasn't on his top ten list of favorite things to do, but it wouldn't come to that. If push came to shove, he'd ask his mother to ask Louis

about the post-office box, and she would do it, much
as Natalie would do things for Adam, without prying.
Furthermore, the fact that he was interested in a
woman would undoubtedly make his mother dance
a little jig of happiness. She'd been delicately laying
hints about him "settling down" and "giving her some
grandchildren." Come to think of it, those hadn't been
delicate hints at all, Levi realized, smiling to himself.

He laughed softly. "You think I've lost my mind,
don't you?"

"No." Adam smiled and released a slow sigh. "But
this chick must be able to write one helluva letter."

"Little brother, you don't know the half of it."

"Oh, I think I know more than you think I do,"
Adam said, his voice low, and with that enigmatic
statement, he stood, gathered his crutches and made
his way into the house.

Levi waited until he'd gone, then withdrew his
wallet and selected the first letter. There had to be a
clue in here somewhere. Something he was missing.
A faint citrus scent wafted from the paper as his
mind soaked up her words, now committed to
memory. Something nagged at him, but he batted the
elusive notion away, lost in her letter once more.

Dear Levi,
If I close my eyes I can see you so clearly. The
lean slope of your cheek, the achingly familiar

curve of your smile. I look at you and my soul recognizes yours. If only yours would do the same....

6

Dear Levi,
Sometimes I dream of just resting my head against your chest and listening to you breathe….

SO MUCH for going to the post office this morning, Natalie thought as she hurried through her shower. After talking to Winnie last night and turning her friend's advice over and over in her head, she hadn't been able to sleep. Rather than lie there in the dark, tossing and turning, she'd done what she normally did when insomnia occasionally struck. A grin stole over her lips.

She'd worked.

The stag was coming along nicely. Though she didn't know precisely why, this piece of art was quickly becoming her favorite. She was more driven, had a clearer vision of what he was supposed to look like than any other project up to this point. There was a grace, a masculinity and an energy about him that was curiously familiar, and yet she couldn't quite put her finger on where that sense of recognition was coming from. The more she worked, the closer she came to figuring it out, and were it not for Levi going with her to the beach this morning, she'd much rather stay home and work on the stag a bit more. As it was…

She quickly lathered and rinsed her hair, then squeezed a bit of her favorite bath gel—Hawaiian Ginger—into her loofah. The scent was fresh and a touch exotic and came from a shop right here in Bethel Bay. She'd been so enchanted with it, she'd bought the lotion and body spray as well. Though her hair could use a bit of conditioner, Natalie decided she'd settle for the spray-in variety this morning. She didn't have time for the traditional method.

Because—she glanced at the clock on her vanity—Levi would be here in exactly thirty-two minutes. Eek, Natalie thought. Though she ordinarily didn't put on makeup and fix her hair to go beach-combing—hell, half the time she only managed to brush her teeth and throw on a ball cap—today she'd decided to make an exception.

If by some bizarre, exceedingly rare chance Levi had been flirting with her yesterday, she didn't want to blow it by looking like a troll. The outfit couldn't change—combing was dirty work—but at the very least she could look presentable and she was just vain enough to want to try.

Natalie turned the water off, grabbed a towel and stepped out of the shower.

It was at that precise moment that she heard her doorbell ring. Panicked, she glanced at the digital clock again. Seven-thirty on the dot. What the— surely he wasn't early, she thought, wrapping the towel around herself. Her heart rate kicked into a swifter rhythm and the toast and jam she'd had for breakfast gave a threatening churn in her belly.

"Hold on!" Natalie called, frantically searching for her robe. Shit. Where had she put it? She darted around her room, kicking yesterday's clothes out of the way, and finally found the worn chenille robe stuffed at the foot of her bed. She dropped the towel, shoved her arms into the garment and belted the sash, then made her way to the front door. A quick view through the privacy hole revealed that it was indeed Levi.

Thirty minutes early.

Pasting a smile on her face, Natalie finally opened the door. "Good morning," she said, a bit breathlessly.

Levi bared his teeth in a grin. "I'm going to kill him," he said.

She blinked. "Kill who?"

"Adam. He told me last night that you'd try to shake me. That I'd better get here early and, fool that I am, I listened to his advice." Looking adorably self-conscious, he jerked a thumb over his shoulder.

"I can come back. Or you can pick me up, as you'd originally suggested. I'll just—"

"Nonsense," Natalie said. She opened the door wider so that he could come in. "You're here now. I'll only be a few more minutes and we can head out."

He shoved his hands into his pockets and gave her a sheepish smile. He wore cargo shorts paired with a brown T-shirt that pulled out the darker flecks in those amazing eyes. A pair of trendy sandals rounded out the outfit. Strangely, he still looked every bit a soldier. A veritable badass. Her belly gave a little flutter and it suddenly occurred to her that she was naked beneath her robe.

Which was the exact moment her nipples pebbled.

His gaze dropped and darkened, before jumping back up and tangling with hers. Levi cleared his throat. "Are you sure?"

The tops of her thighs burned. "Certainly. Come on in."

She moved aside, allowing him over the threshold. Two steps later, he paused, sniffing the air. Something shifted in those toffee-colored eyes. "You smell nice."

"Thanks. It's a fragrance from Bayside Soap Company. I try to buy from our local vendors and I happen to really like this scent."

His gaze sharpened. "Local, you say?"

It seemed an odd question, but she answered anyway. "Yes. The Wintermans have operated the company for the past three generations. They've recently added candles to their stock." She gestured to the one sitting on her coffee table.

He smiled, but it seemed a bit awkward and left her with the impression that she was missing something. "I, uh…I should pick up one for Mom."

"I'm sure she'd like that. Can I get you something to drink? Tea? Coffee?"

Levi shook his head. "No thanks. I'm good." He glanced around her ground floor. "You've got a beautiful place here."

A blush of pleasure moved through her. "Thanks. It suits my purposes."

"Do you mind if I look around while you finish getting ready? I'd really like to see that studio Adam mentioned."

"Not at all. Make yourself at home."

Exactly seven minutes later, after aiming the hair dryer at her head for a couple of minutes and an obligatory swipe of the mascara wand, Natalie found him in her studio, admiring the stag. Seeing him next to the piece—the angle of his head, the breadth of his shoulders, the very way he stood—felt strangely like déjà vu, and when he looked up, recognition bolted through her.

He was the stag.

Sweet Lord, how could she have missed it? How could she—

"Natalie, this is beyond amazing," he said, an unbelievably beautiful smile sliding over those sinfully crafted lips. Morning light spilled in from the floor-to-ceiling windows, bathing him in a golden glow, glinting off that light brown—almost fawn-like—hair. Desire and longing broadsided her, making her knees go weak and her breath go shallow. Every depraved scenario she'd written to him flitted rapid-fire through her mind, a little mini-porn show of her own desires. Them naked and tangled in her sheets, him taking her against her front door, her sliding her hands over his perfect flesh, his fingers threaded through hers…

Without warning, Winnie's advice came back to her. *What if this is it? What if this is your only chance? Are you going to waste it trying to intercept a letter?*

Natalie swallowed hard. No, she wasn't.

"Thank you," she finally managed to say, though it was damned difficult. Struggling to gather her composure, she strolled over to join him and pretended to admire the way the stag was coming together. "I worked on him until three this morning."

A line formed between Levi's brows and he looked confused. "This is going to sound crazy, but there's something familiar about him." He glanced at the doe. "Her, too." He shook his head. "But the stag… It's strange. I get the feeling that I should recognize him."

It was all she could do to keep her lips from twitching. "I'm glad. The true measure of all art isn't just that we appreciate it, but that we can identify with it as well."

He arched a skeptical brow. "You mean I'm identifying with your deer?"

She grinned. "In a manner of speaking. It's making you *feel*, right?"

"Gets me right in the chest," he murmured, putting a fist against his.

Her, too, Natalie thought. Every time she looked at him. Or more importantly, at Levi.

A sheepish smile slid over his lips and he rubbed a hand over the back of his neck. "I hope you don't take this the wrong way…but I had no idea you were this talented. It was really a shock yesterday to see all those things in your gallery."

A bark of laughter broke from her throat and she rolled her eyes. "Thank you. I think."

"No, no," he said, as though he were making a mess of things. "Damn, I'm not good at this. It was— *is*—a compliment. You've truly got a gift."

Natalie nodded, moved beyond words. She'd been lauded in various magazines and art circles, had participated in gallery showings from L.A. to New York, and had been blessed with more than a few celebrity clients, but curiously, Levi's backhanded compliment meant more to her than any of those things ever could.

He glanced around the room and gestured toward the various bins stacked with driftwood. A hint of a grin tugged at the corner of his mouth. "And no shortage of your material, either."

No doubt he was wondering why she liked to go to the beach every day, Natalie thought. She smiled, a bit self-consciously. "It would seem so, but I'm always afraid I'm going to miss that special piece, that perfect part I'm going to need to make something come together."

He nodded knowingly and crossed his arms over his chest. "Ah, I see." He grinned. "Sort of."

Natalie chuckled. "It's a quirk, I'll admit. But…" She shrugged helplessly. "It's the method to my madness."

Admiration along with something else, something less easily defined, sparked in that golden gaze. "It's obviously working." He straightened. "Speaking of which, we should probably get going."

Right, Natalie thought. It was time to get going… on a relationship that could go nowhere.

But, perversely, she looked forward to the ride.

WHILE Natalie paused to chat with a couple on the beach, Levi took the opportunity to call his brother and ream his ass.

"Lying bastard," he hissed into the phone.

Adam chuckled. "What? Is there a problem?"

"She was home, dickweed," Levi said. "Just like you knew she would be."

Home and naked and moist, and my God, she'd smelled like heaven. Had been floating in the same citrusly scent that accompanied each and every one of his letters from Ms. X. A local product, one that could be used by any of Bethel Bay's residents, and yet…

Levi let his gaze drift over Natalie. Damn, she was gorgeous. Lean and lightly tanned. He loved the pert angle of her nose, the adorable stubborn tilt to her chin. And that mouth. Absolutely the sexiest thing he'd ever seen.

This morning when she'd opened the door, it had been all he could do not to walk right in and devour her, take her hard and fast against her door, just like the description in his most recent letter from his hometown admirer. Natalie had been the one he'd been thinking of when he'd read the letter in the first place, so seeing her this morning was just heaping temptation on an already tempting situation. Between those deep-brown eyes—eyes that seemed to see right through him, *know* him—and that luscious mouth…

Dear God, how was he going to resist her?

"She'd just gotten out of the shower," Levi told him, instantly going hard again. "I looked like a damned fool."

"She looks good wet, doesn't she?"

"What?"

"Natalie looks good wet. She might be my friend, but I'm allowed to recognize sexy. Lots of girls can't pull it off. No makeup, hair plastered to their heads." He made a sound of disgust. "But not Natalie. She doesn't need makeup and she's got the bone structure to make it work. And her hair. Brings out the caveman tendencies, doesn't it?"

Had he lost his friggin' mind? Levi wondered. What sort of conversation was this? "Adam, I don't know what the hell you're playing at, but I'm about to—"

"—make a play for her, I hope," Adam interjected cheerfully. "Hell, Levi, it's obvious that you're interested in her. Why don't you stop pussyfooting around and man up?"

Shit. A shock of disbelief followed quickly by quiet acceptance moved through him. How long had Adam known? "Who said I—"

"Nobody had to say it. I can just tell. I've always been able to tell, even when you were trying to shackle yourself to that frigid, unfaithful slut. I tried to talk to you about it then, but you wouldn't listen to me."

True, Levi remembered. Adam had never liked Sabrina and had made many veiled references to her being the wrong girl for him. He'd sure as hell been right about that. Could he be right about Natalie as well?

"I'm not exactly sure what you're waiting on," Adam continued, "but if it's my permission, then you've got it, okay? Stop wasting time. You're only home for a week. Make the best of it." He chuckled, but his voice had developed an edge. "Just don't hurt her or I'll have to kick your ass."

Levi gave a grim laugh and his gaze slid to Natalie. Another firecracker of heat detonated in his loins. "Those are conflicting orders, little brother. If I make the best of it, you know she's going to get hurt when I leave."

"Natalie's a big girl. She knows how you feel about your career. She's not going to ask you for a damned thing you don't want to give."

She looked so beautiful standing by the water. She was smiling, her face alight with laughter, a piece of driftwood in her hand. A soft breeze toyed with the ends of her hair. *Caveman tendencies* was right, Levi decided. He'd like nothing more than to wrap his hand in her hair, drag her back to her house and make love to her until his balls burst or he died, whichever came first.

"What makes you think she's interested?" Since Adam's intuition had been dead on with him, it only stood to reason that he knew Natalie well enough to pick up the vibe from her. Still…

Adam hesitated. "It's just a feeling I've got."

Not good enough. He didn't want to make a play

for her, only to have it backfire. Talk about awkward. She was one of his brother's best friends. She wouldn't simply "go away" when this was over. And, eventually, it would have to end. He had a career he loved and she had a home she wouldn't want to leave. "I don't know if I want to risk humiliation based on 'just a feeling,'" Levi continued. "You're going to have to do better than that." For whatever reason, he got the distinct impression that Adam was holding back on him. His hesitation practically screamed across the line.

Adam released a pent-up breath. "I think she's your Ms. X," he finally admitted.

Shock jolted through him. *"What?"*

"I've suspected it for a while, but she's never said anything, and I kept asking to see the damned letters so that I could compare the handwriting to the ones I'd been getting from her—which incidentally happened to arrive on the same day *your* letters did. But you wouldn't let me see them, you stubborn ass, so—"

"I thought you were just being a nosy bastard," Levi growled threateningly. "If I'd had any idea you might know who they were coming from I would have let you see them!"

His raised voice attracted attention, most notably Natalie's. Her brow knitted with questioning concern. He offered her a reassuring smile, then turned and continued to hiss into the phone at his brother.

"I can't believe you've kept this from me. What the hell were you thinking?"

"I was thinking that it was fun," Adam said. "I like rattling your cage. Besides, I wasn't sure how you would feel about the letters being from Natalie. I wasn't sure you were still into her, you know? If you weren't, then I didn't want to ruin it for you. But after seeing you with her yesterday…I dunno." His sigh echoed over the line. "I just hate to see either of you squander this opportunity. Life's short and you and I know that better than most people do."

He was right. Still…

"You're sure they're from her?"

"No, I'm not," Adam clarified. "I have a very strong suspicion that they are."

"What about the letters she's written to you? Do you have them so that we can compare?"

"Not all of my stuff is here yet," Adam told him. "But I would recognize her handwriting if you want to show me any of your letters."

Levi hesitated, torn. He didn't want to share the letters—they were private. She'd written them to him, not to anyone else, and somehow the idea of sharing any part of them, even with Adam, felt like a betrayal of her trust.

He couldn't do it, Levi decided. As much as he wanted to know for certain whether or not Natalie was Ms. X…he couldn't do it.

Adam chuckled knowingly. "Noble bastard."

"You just want to read the letters."

"I'd give my· left nut to read those damned letters," his brother freely admitted, startling a laugh out of Levi.

"Yeah, well, save your nut because you're not going to get so much as a peek at them."

His gaze slid to Natalie once more. Could it be her? Levi wondered. Was it possible that Adam was right? Or was it merely wishful thinking?

While his manipulative, greedy subconscious had dubbed her into the starring role, the idea that it could really be her was almost surreal. Almost more than he dared to hope for.

And it also gave a whole new meaning to every word she'd written. Every dream, every fantasy.

They were *hers…of him*.

He went hard just thinking about it.

Could it really be her? he wondered again, almost afraid to hope.

A slow grin slid over Levi's lips as a plan surfaced in his reeling brain. His letter writer typically checked mail around four, eh?

In that case, a trip to the post office this ·afternoon—*together*—was in order.

7

Dear Levi,
I found a piece of beach glass this morning the exact shade of your eyes. I've suspended it from a length of fishing line and hung it in my bedroom window…

NATALIE NODDED at the lavender box sitting on the table next to Adam. "Winnie came by?"

Adam consulted his cards, purposely, it seemed, avoiding her gaze. "She did. She brought me some of those little cakes and cookies." He nodded approvingly. "Good stuff."

"She makes the best in town," Natalie said, pleased that Winnie had made this first step. She determinedly looked at her own cards, trying not to ogle Levi, who was currently painting over the *Sabrina* with a coat of heavy-duty white paint.

Considering he was shirtless, it was damned hard.

Muscles bunched beneath gleaming, surprisingly

tanned skin and she was hit with the almost over-whelming urge to lick the fluted hollow of his spine, to run her hands over the intriguing landscape of his chest. Even his neck was sexy, particularly the little soft part just below his ear. Her belly grew all hot and muddled and a tingle of heat washed over her breasts. Natalie released a shaky breath. Good Lord, the man was beautiful. Literally, truly beautiful. And—

"Natalie?"

She started and felt a blush rush to her hairline. "Oh, is it my turn?"

Adam grinned at her in a way that made her distinctly uncomfortable. He jerked his head toward Levi. "I know he's not much to look at, Nat, but staring at him like he's a circus freak isn't polite." If his tongue was planted any more firmly in his cheek it would have to be surgically removed, the smart ass.

"I wasn't s-staring," she lied, hoping a rogue bolt of lightning wouldn't strike.

He shrugged. "Looked to me like you were staring. And that little slurping noise you made—" He winced, leaving the rest unspoken.

She gasped, outraged. She knew damned well she hadn't made a slurping noise. At least, she was relatively certain she hadn't. Natalie chuckled, trying to keep from throwing up.

He knew.

"You're so full of shit," she said, then gestured to

his cards. "Just play, would you? We've only got a few more minutes."

"Yeah, yeah. I know. You and Levi are going back to the beach." There was a very vague sense of envy in his voice, which made her heart ache. Though she knew he put on a brave front, her friend was hurting and, other than being there for him, she was powerless to help. "He said you found a lot of good pieces this morning."

"We did," she confirmed. "I really appreciate him telling Dad he'd go with me. He wouldn't have agreed to go to Uncle Milton's otherwise."

"I know he's your dad, Nat, and I understand why he's worried about you, but…"

"I know," she said, sighing. "I've let it go too far." Her poor father had called twice already today to check on her. She hated that he worried so much. He truly had to come to terms with the fact that she would be fine. "And, strictly speaking, I can go alone," she continued. "I've told Levi that, but he insists that he come along. Says he gave his word to my dad." A man who kept his word, she thought, her lips twisting. A novel change. Of course, she wouldn't expect anything else from Levi.

A dry bark of laughter erupted from Adam. "If he gave his word, there's no way in hell he won't go with you. But if you're thinking he volunteered for the job just for your father's sake, you'd better think again."

Natalie's mouth went bone-dry, her head felt light and her heart began to pound.

Adam tossed another card down, then leaned forward and shot her a grin. "I think he's into you. And I think you're his Mysterious Ms. X."

That was it—her chicken salad was coming back up. Natalie bolted from her chair. "Excuse me," she said, putting her hand over her mouth as she hurried to the bathroom.

Three minutes later, after she'd emptied the contents of her stomach and come to terms with the fact that Adam was apparently psychic, she made her way back outside to argue with him on both counts.

But she couldn't. Because Levi had finished his paint job and returned to the back porch. He was just shrugging into his shirt—more's the pity—and his caramel gaze met hers as she walked out.

"You okay?" he asked, concern lining his brow.

"Fine," Natalie said, her eyes swinging to a completely unrepentant Adam who was smiling so smugly she was inclined to pummel him with his own crutches.

"Adam said you'd gotten sick."

She glared at Adam. "My lunch didn't agree with me."

"Nothing agrees with you when you get nervous, does it, Nat?" he needled.

She genuinely wanted to throttle him.

"It's like a little truth barometer, isn't it?" Adam shook his head, seemingly pondering the magical properties of her nervous stomach.

Levi's gaze jumped back and forth between the two of them. "Am I missing something?"

"Just a chromosome or two, but it's nothing to worry about." Adam glanced at his watch. "I thought you were going to the post office today?"

Levi nodded and an unreadable look passed over his too-handsome face. His gaze found hers and he quirked a brow. "Do you mind if we swing by the post office before going down to the beach? I'm expecting a letter."

It was a good thing her stomach was empty, Natalie thought as she pasted a wholly unnatural smile onto her face. "Not at all."

Adam's lips twitched infuriatingly. "Nat, have you chosen a chick flick yet?"

Oh, she'd get him back. "As a matter of fact, I have. You haven't seen *Love, Actually,* have you?" Colin Firth, Liam Neeson, Hugh Grant, Alan Rickman. She inwardly sighed. It was the motherlode of movie stars.

"I haven't."

She nodded once and resisted the urge to preen. "Excellent. I'll see you at seven."

He idly threaded his fingers and put them behind his head, stretching. "Are you making your lasagna?"

"I can." But only because she knew how much he liked it. Honestly, he was shameless.

"Good. I'm sure Levi will enjoy it."

A flutter of panic whipped through her chest, and from the corner of her eye she saw Levi arch a brow.

"Why would I enjoy it?" he asked.

"Remember how you said if there was anything you could do for me, just to name it?"

Seemingly suspecting a trap, Levi nodded cautiously. "I remember."

"I'm naming it." Adam jerked his head toward Natalie. "I want you to watch the chick flick in my place." He rubbed his thigh, playing the ultimate sympathy card. "I'm going to be too tired to go to her house and watch a movie."

Natalie felt a disbelieving smile slide over her lips. He was the devil. The spawn of Satan incarnate. And so bloody obvious she wanted to crawl into a hole. "Too tired to watch a movie? Really?"

Though Adam sighed heavily, a twinkle lit his eyes. "Yes, I'm afraid so. I've got therapy in the morning, so I need to conserve my strength."

As much as she would love Levi to come over for dinner and a movie, she didn't want him maneuvered into it and she didn't want to take any more time away from his family. He was already spending a couple of hours in the morning and evening with her. It hardly seemed fair to let Adam—well-intentioned as her interfering friend was, she thought exasperatedly—impose his chick-flick penalty on Levi as well.

"What about your mom and dad?" Natalie asked. "Don't you think they'd like him to stay home?"

"They've got their ballroom-dancing class tonight," Adam said. A wide smile split his face. "They'll be gone for hours. Besides, they'll see him tomorrow. Other than hanging out with you, he's spending every minute with them. They'll understand."

"Sounds like you've thought this through," Levi remarked, studying his brother carefully.

Adam snorted. "Anything to get out of watching *Love, Actually.*"

"What?" Natalie asked. "Afraid you'll cry again?"

Adam instantly bristled. "I didn't cry, dammit. I told you I had something in my eye."

Natalie looked at Levi. "It's true. He did. It's called a tear."

Levi chuckled and she felt that sexy laugh all the way to the bottoms of her feet. She loved the way his eyes crinkled at the corners, the faint dimple in his left cheek when he smiled. She was hit with an inexplicable impulse to lean in, to move closer to him. He smelled like ocean and man, a tang of sea salt and a woodsy fragrance all his own. Her toes actually curled.

"Smart ass," Adam grumbled.

"Damn, bro. If you're afraid you'll cry, I don't mind watching the movie for you." Humor danced in Levi's toffee-gaze. "I'll take one for the team." He looked at Natalie and the glimpse of heat she caught in his eyes made her momentarily lose her breath. "Can I bring anything?" Levi asked her. "A bottle of wine, maybe?"

Wine? she thought as her pulse tripped wildly in her veins. If he'd offered to bring dessert or a salad or anything else, she could have written it off as being polite. This was the South after all. You didn't show up to any sort of social event empty-handed. It wasn't done.

But offering to bring wine indicated a change in the status quo, a plan to take things up a level. It smacked of something much more intentional and romantic.

Something like, Lord help her, *a date.*

AT TEN minutes before seven, Levi found his brother parked in front of the television, idly flipping channels. He looked bored to tears and there was a haunted expression in his eyes that made Levi long to fix things for him, to make things right. Unfortunately, he didn't know how. For the first time in his life, he wasn't sure what his brother needed.

"I know what you're trying to do and I appreciate it," Levi said, watching Adam frown before biting into another one of those cookies he'd been munching on all day. "But why don't you come down to Natalie's with me? Forget the movie and we'll just hang out. Play cards or whatever."

"I'll have plenty of time to hang out with Natalie after you're gone."

Too true, Levi thought. At the end of the week he'd be boarding a return flight to Iraq. He'd be back with his boys, back to what was familiar.

Because being here with Natalie was anything but familiar.

This intense desire, this bone-deep, unbelievable ache to spend every waking—and non-waking—second with her, the almost blinding, driving need to bury himself between her thighs…there was absolutely nothing familiar about that.

He'd never wanted a woman as much as he wanted her.

It was the strangest thing. Once he'd fully admitted to himself the depth of his desire, it was as though the admission had triggered a landslide of emotion—of need—inside him that threatened to wash away anything that even remotely resembled common sense or restraint. And whatever shred he'd managed to hold on to had completely vanished with Adam's approval and his insight into Natalie being Ms. X.

Honestly, Levi had never looked at a woman and felt this mind-boggling ache in his chest while his nether regions experienced the fiery hell of the damned. It was strange and wonderful, and looking at her made him wonder if he'd been too premature in deciding that there wasn't room in his life for a wife *and* his career.

This afternoon while he'd gone over to the post office, Natalie had insisted on dropping by the gallery to check on things, citing an incompetent assistant and things that needed her attention. He knew she was purposely avoiding going to the post office with him, and more than ever, he was convinced that Adam was right.

She'd been writing the letters.

He felt it in his gut.

After listening to the sound of her voice, the cadence of her speech, he could "hear her," for lack of a better description, when he read the letters. Though nothing had arrived from her in today's mail, he had gotten a few items—bills and such—so things were definitely being forwarded. It was a small comfort. He knew that another letter had to be coming, otherwise she wouldn't be so damned nervous. If she hadn't been the one writing to him, then why had she acted like a spooked cat when he'd tried to get her to walk over to the post office with him?

It *had* to be her.

This afternoon, after beachcombing with her for about an hour, he'd come home, and he and Adam had taken his newly unnamed boat out for a short spin. While Adam had lazed around on deck, Levi had taken the time to read back through the letters and had found what he thought was a pretty good clue. In one of her letters, she'd described the view from her living room over the water. There were lots of waterfront properties in Bethel Bay, but very few had a weeping cherry tree in the yard.

He knew because he'd looked today.

Point of fact, gut-feeling and wishful thinking aside, there were too many little things that suggested Natalie was his Mysterious Ms. X. The ginger-citrus scent that accompanied each one of the letters, the fact that she'd thrown up when Adam had point blank told her that he thought she was his Mysterious Ms. X—a curiously endearing quirk—and her reticence to join him at the post office. He was ninety-nine-point-nine percent positive that she was responsible for the letters, and the instant the next missive came, he had a feeling he was going to know for certain.

In the meantime he intended to do exactly what his brother had suggested—he was going for it.

Whether or not Natalie turned out to be Ms. X, he wanted her. He'd wanted her from the instant he'd seen her dancing around their driveway to the tune of "Sweet Child of Mine" and, though he'd kept his distance and tried to replace her with someone else, had come up with and used many arguments to keep from pursuing her…the time for that was at an end.

Something about Natalie had always drawn him. Intense physical attraction aside, he could honestly say he simply loved being around her. She had the unique ability to simultaneously energize and relax him. As Adam had so eloquently pointed out, she was easy company. She had a fantastic sense of humor, alternately wry and outrageous, was incredibly talented, loyal to her friends, her town and heritage, and genuinely…did it for him.

Furthermore, though this made no sense given the fact that he loved traveling and enjoyed living in different places, Levi suspected that the thing that truly drew him to her was the fact that she was so…*grounded*.

Natalie Rowland knew her place in the world, her position here in the local scheme of things. She had roots, Levi thought, and despite the fact that he'd rather sow wild oats from one end of the globe to the other, there was something distinctly comforting in that.

"You're sure you don't want to go?" Levi asked his brother again.

Adam looked up. "Absolutely." He paused. "You'll be good together."

Levi silently agreed, then grabbed the wine he'd picked up from town and took his leave. The short walk to Natalie's door was probably one of the longest he'd ever traversed and he was unaccountably nervous.

He'd fought terrorists, dammit, and his hands hadn't so much as shaken. Yet at the moment his insides were vibrating so hard he could barely swallow.

It boggled the mind.

And, of course, now that he was relatively certain she was Ms. X, Levi knew he wasn't going to be able to look at her without imagining each and every one of those fantasies she'd written to him about.

He wanted to reenact them. In the flesh.

The mouthwatering scent of lasagna washed over him the instant she opened her door. Natalie wore a pale-yellow-and-white polka-dotted sundress and she'd left her hair down so it fell in soft waves over her shoulders and slithered down her back. Plain diamond studs winked in her small ears and the smile stretching across her elfin face was nothing short of breathtaking. It was also a bit unsure, which he found curiously endearing. Just like those freckles scattered over her pert nose.

She was beautiful. Quite possibly the loveliest creature he'd ever seen. And the kicker? The thing that just set him off like a firecracker on the Fourth of July?

She had no idea.

He held up the bottle of wine. "Your booze, milady."

Natalie laughed. "I happen to like chick flicks. You're the one who's going to need to self-medicate with the alcohol."

She accepted the wine and gestured for him to

follow her into the kitchen. Naturally he couldn't do it without looking at her ass and damn... Though the fabric of her dress wasn't see-through, he could make out what he instinctively knew was a thong. A band of sweat broke out over his upper lip.

Clearly she was trying to kill him.

Levi sighed and shook his head. "So you're going to hold me to it, eh?"

Natalie withdrew a corkscrew from a drawer and handed it to him. "You do the honors, would you? And, of course, I'm not going to hold you to the movie." She rolled her eyes. "Adam's the one who owes me the chick flick, not you. You can read the back of the DVD box and *pretend* you've seen it."

Levi chuckled. "Very crafty. I like that in a woman. So what are we going to do then?"

He could think of lots of things and none of them included watching a movie. For starters, now that he'd decided to seriously make a play for her, he'd like nothing better than to kiss her. His gaze lingered over her lips. He wanted to taste those raspberry lips, feel her tongue against his. He wanted to push his fingers into her hair and feel it slide over the backs of his hands. He wanted to set her on the counter, lift the dress and make dinner of her. Eat, sample and savor every part of her.

And because of her letters, he knew she wanted it, too.

Natalie opened the oven door. The groan of pleasure she gave at the delicious aroma that wafted out affected him on a visceral level. She grabbed a couple of pot holders from the counter and withdrew the bubbling dish, then set it on top of the stove.

"We're going to eat and watch a movie, just not the one Adam thinks we're watching."

He poured them each a glass of wine, strolled over and handed one to her. He purposely invaded her space—if she had any doubts about his intentions and what he wanted, he'd disabuse her of those right now—and had the pleasure of watching her pulse flutter wildly at the base of her throat. Mission accomplished, Levi thought, pleased.

"And what are we really going to see?"

"The Shining," Natalie said, shocking the hell out of him as she accepted her drink.

A startled laugh rumbled from his chest. *"The Shining?* Really?" What? Was *Psycho* already rented?

Her dark gaze met his, then dropped to his lips. She absently licked hers and he went hard. "I've, uh…I've always wanted to see it and am too much of a wuss to watch it alone." She quirked a brow. "Is that okay with you?"

Only if she ended up in his lap, Levi thought. And somehow he imagined that was the whole point. Good food, good company, wine and a horror flick.

It was the perfect first date.

He smiled down at her. "It's totally fine with me. But I'll warn you. You may have to hold my hand."

8

Dear Levi,
I love the way your mouth hitches up into that
little half-grin. It makes my heart skip a
beat…and my nipples tingle…

HE HADN'T BEEN kidding about the holding his hand
thing, Natalie thought as Levi's strong fingers lay
entwined with hers on top of his muscled thigh. A
sexual current seemed to run from his fingers through
hers and straight to the very heart of her sex. They
sat in a sort of expectant silence as the final credits
rolled.

"*Damn,*" Levi finally said, releasing a pent-up
breath. "That was one scary ass movie."

Understatement of the year, Natalie thought.
She'd heard about the legendary horror film for
years, but had never watched it. Levi hadn't either,
which had made her self-serving, give-her-a-reason-
to-cuddle selection perfect.

Natalie grinned. "Are you saying you'd rather have watched the chick flick?" she teased.

"Hell no," Levi said, chuckling. He squeezed her hand. "This was nice. I haven't watched a movie in ages."

"I love movies," she admitted. "They're one of my favorite forms of entertainment."

A wicked twinkle lit his eyes and it was obvious he was thinking about a completely different form of entertainment. The kind that involved naked skin and hurried breathing and culminated with a back-clawing, toe-curling release. "I enjoy it, but I don't think I'd go so far as to say it was one of my favorites. I prefer a more…physical form of entertainment." His gaze caught and held hers. "Unless it's reading, of course. Particularly letters."

Oh, hell. Natalie swallowed as her stomach gave an ominous quiver.

"Did Adam mention that I've been getting letters from a woman from Bethel Bay?" he asked, studying her closely.

"He, er… He might have mentioned it." She'd known this was coming, that it was only a matter of time before he'd bring it up. And she should own up, Natalie thought. Get it out of the way. Just tell him. This deception had gone on long enough.

All she had to do was admit that she was his Mysterious Ms. X and they could move forward, in the admittedly temporary direction they both wanted. Though she didn't know whether Adam had shared his suspicions with Levi, given the leading questions he'd asked she knew he had his own incriminating thoughts on the subject as well.

And just because he didn't know now for sure didn't mean he wouldn't know shortly. That letter with her return address would be here any day, and when it came...

She should just tell him, Natalie thought again, trying to drum up the nerve to do just that.

But she couldn't. Ridiculous and cowardly, she knew, but—

"I've really appreciated them," Levi told her, twisting the guilt knife even further. A faint smile tugged at the corner of his mouth. "They've uh... They've meant a lot."

"That's nice," Natalie said, for lack of anything better. Meanwhile her heart did a little pirouette.

She'd known that he'd been smitten with her letters—had enjoyed them—because he'd written her back and told her so. Told her that and so much more. Those letters had opened the line of communication between them and the intimacy they'd created—even anonymously—had been nothing short of magical. She'd poured out her heart, but had measured and selected each word with care.

Levi waited, evidently for her to confess, and let out a silent, almost imperceptible sigh when she didn't.

"It's getting late," he finally said. "I should get going." Still holding her hand, he reluctantly stood and made his way to the door. He stared down at her. "Dinner was fabulous," he murmured. He edged closer, leaving no room for doubt about his intentions. "Adam was right about your lasagna."

He's going to kiss me, Natalie thought faintly. *Finally, finally, finally, after all these years.* Her lips tingled in anticipation, her breasts grew heavy, and a steady insistent warmth pooled in her middle.

"Much as it pains me to admit it, Adam is usually right about a lot of things. I think the world of your brother. He's one of my best friends."

His measured gaze searched hers. "I kept thinking the two of you would become more than friends."

Natalie laughed. "You and everybody else." She let go a breath and shook her head. "But we've never been interested in each other that way." Though she wasn't about to admit it to Levi, she and Adam had even kissed once to test the waters. Nothing, nada, zilch. Her gaze inexplicably dropped to his lips and a bolt of heat hit her womb. "There's never been any chemistry."

He sidled closer, incinerating her with his nearness. A flash of goosebumps skittered up her spine and camped at the back of her neck. "Chemistry's important."

Sweet Lord, he smelled good. Natalie licked her lips. "Essential," she said.

That melting caramel gaze traced every line in her face and settled hungrily on her mouth. "I happen to think that we've got it."

He's killing me, Natalie thought. *Absolutely killing me.* "You do?"

Another wicked chuckle, then "In spades." He tugged her closer and bent his head until his lips were just a hairbreadth away from her own. "Do you feel it?" he whispered huskily.

She nodded because she couldn't speak. God help her, if she felt it any more she'd self-combust.

He smiled, ever so slightly, the wretch. He knew what he was doing to her, knew that she wanted him more than she wanted her next breath. In fact, breathing seemed highly overrated at the moment. She'd completely forgotten how to do it.

And then his lips finally, blessedly—she even heard faint tones of the hallelujah chorus—touched hers and the air she'd been holding inexplicably leaked out in a sigh of utter and complete pleasure. It was as though every minute of her life was tied to this particular second, as though every tick of the clock had been leading up to the mating of their mouths, to the instant when he would kiss her. Sound receded. Sensation reigned. Happiness and joy the likes of which she'd never known, and instinctively knew she'd never recognize again, rushed through in waves of euphoria so intense she could scarcely believe it.

Levi made a soft growl of masculine pleasure as his lips brushed lightly—almost reverently—over her mouth. Once, twice, a sampling, and then his hands framed her face, pushed into her hair, and her soldier, her badass, her hero, the bona fide love of her life, *laid siege.*

There was no other term for it.

His tongue tangled around hers in a thorough exploration of the soft recesses of her mouth. He tasted like wine and marinara, like rain after a long drought. Like heaven, Natalie thought dimly. Even better than Winnie's petits fours and that was saying something.

His thumb stroked her cheek in an achingly tender gesture, as though he'd been waiting a lifetime for this as well, and he fed at her mouth, suckling, tasting, deepening the kiss until her legs shook and her knees threatened to give way. She leaned closer, absorbing the hot, hard feel of him against her, then carefully entwined her arms around his neck.

She loved the feel of his close-cropped hair against her fingers and slid the pad of her thumb behind the curiously vulnerable patch of soft skin just below and behind his ear. *Soft, vulnerable.* Descriptions that should have been at odds with such masculinity, but were, quite strangely, perfect.

"Do you have any idea how long I've wanted to do this?" Levi asked, a hint of desperation in his gravelly voice. His hands slid purposefully down her back and settled hotly over her rump.

"Not nearly as long as I've wanted you to, I'll bet," Natalie told him, her giddy heart giving a little jump in her chest. She suckled his bottom lip, wanting to kiss other parts of him. Neck and shoulder, chest and abdomen…and parts farther south. A particular part that was currently nudging impatiently—gratifyingly—against her middle.

Levi rested his forehead against hers. "Years," he said.

She drew back, shocked. *Years?* Really? But she'd never detected— She'd never imagined— Years? "What the hell was the hold-up?"

"I've told you already. I thought you and Adam would eventually become a 'thing' and I didn't want to tread into my brother's territory."

He wouldn't, she knew. It made perfect sense. And yet… "What about Sabrina?"

He chuckled darkly. "A poor substitute, a mistake, a monumental lapse in judgment. Need I go on?" He gave his head a shake. "I don't know what the hell I was thinking."

"I don't know what the hell you were thinking, either. She was all wrong for you."

He grinned, seemingly pleased with her assessment. "And I suppose you know what's right for me?"

Natalie felt her cheeks warm. "I think I've got a better grasp of it than she ever did, yes." *She* was right for him, thank you very much.

Levi drew back a bit once again and seemed to hesitate. "Adam has threatened to kick my ass if I hurt you."

Translation—*this is temporary, I'm only home for a few more days, my career comes first, and this will never be more than it is right now.*

He didn't have to say it. She'd known it all along. And it was good enough, Natalie thought. It had to be. She'd rather have him now—for whatever amount of time they had—than miss the opportunity altogether. She'd deal with the fallout later.

Natalie leaned forward and gently kissed the corner of his mouth, not the least bit surprised that he'd addressed the elephant in the room before taking things any further. It was noble and right and heroic. She inwardly smiled.

It was *so* Levi.

Which was why she'd lie. "You're not going to hurt me, Levi." She didn't have *any* expectations beyond this week. "I know what we're doing."

THEN THAT MAKES ONE OF US, Levi thought. Because he sure as hell didn't know what he was doing.

He'd thought he did…until he'd kissed her.

Then every bit of gray matter he possessed seemed to vanish and it had just been his lips on hers, her lithe body pressed tightly against his. Those talented fingers that created unique and wonderful works of art sliding over the back of his neck and into his hair, tracing the shell of his ear. It had conversely soothed and enflamed him, made his chest go tight and his heart do a funny little thump against his ribcage.

Though it was the most profound and provocative kiss of his life, it had also been…more. Something less easily defined and more *felt*. He was certain this emotion had some sort of name, but absolutely refused to label it. Shameful cowardice, particularly for a so-called badass Ranger, but so be it. He'd rather take an unknown hill than admit what he suspected he was feeling for Natalie.

The hill was a lot less terrifying.

Levi had been kissing girls since grade school, having sex on a semi-routine basis since his sophomore year. No brag, just fact, but he'd been charming the pants off practically any girl he'd set his sights on since puberty. Some had fallen willingly into his arms, some had required more persuading.

Seducing a woman had always come fairly easily to him. A slow smile, an I'm-into-you up-nod and it was usually game on. He never made any promises and made sure that the women he kept company with knew the rules going in. Though some guys were a little less than truthful when it came to bed sport, Levi preferred the honest, direct approach. It gave the lady in question the option to refuse, should she not agree to the terms.

And frankly, there were too many women looking for the same one-night relationship to muddy the waters with a woman who wasn't. No muss, no fuss. Everybody walked away happy and mutually satisfied, without feeling used.

Given Levi's typical *modus operandi*, Adam had been fully justified in issuing the warning on Natalie's behalf. The problem was…who was going to issue a warning on *his* behalf?

Because for the first time in his life, he suspected he was going to need one.

Kissing Natalie had been different. Better. More. It honestly defied description, and if he came apart with a mere meeting of the mouths, then what the hell was going to happen to him when he finally made love to her? When he finally settled himself firmly between her thighs?

Though she still hadn't admitted that she was his Mysterious Ms. X, he knew it all the same and was proceeding accordingly. They only had a small window of opportunity to be together and he'd be damned if he'd waste it chasing what he knew in his gut was a foregone conclusion.

It was her.

And thanks to those letters he had an inside track to her dreams and desires. He knew what she wanted—most importantly, him—and how she wanted it and when she wanted it. His imagination had cast her into those graphic scenes she'd written to him and, as a result, he'd been cocked, locked and ready to rock since the first letter had arrived.

He'd read those fantasies over and over—sometimes to the point that he'd had to take matters into his own hands, so to speak—and now he'd been given the rare opportunity to live them out.

In the flesh.

With her.

Unfortunately he'd fly out of Charlotte on Saturday morning. That gave him only four days to make a lifetime's worth of her—and his—sexual fantasies come true.

"We've wasted a lot of time," Levi told her, content for the moment just to hold her.

She winced. "I know."

"I don't want to waste any more."

Her laugh tickled his neck. "You won't get any objection from me. Although I hate the idea of taking time away from your family."

Levi shrugged. "Just because I'm home doesn't mean their lives are on hold. I'll spend time with them while you're at work."

"How will they feel about this? We won't be able to keep it a secret."

"Whatever makes me happy makes them happy," Levi said. Which was true in the general sense. No doubt his mother would be imagining a wedding and grandchildren, Levi thought, surprised when he didn't involuntarily recoil. Because it would be Natalie meeting him at the altar and red-haired, brown-eyed babies and…

Damn.

She made a noise, seemingly satisfied with his answer, then brushed a kiss against the underside of his jaw, setting off a blast of heat in his groin. She slipped one hand over the back of his neck and the other at the base of his spine, pressing herself more tightly to him. It was slow and leisurely, demanding and erotic, and it stoked the flame inside him to a fever pitch.

Though he knew he should go before things got too far out of control—because when things ultimately went out of control, it was going to be one of her made-to-order fantasies—Levi couldn't help himself. His legs were rooted to the spot and his hands had taken on a life of their own. They were determined to slip and slide all over Natalie's body. They slid down her ribcage, around her back and settled over her magnificent ass.

How long had he wanted to do that? Levi wondered,

as he filled his palms with her sweetly curved rump. How long had he wanted to suckle her ripe bottom lip, exactly the way he was doing now, or pull her tongue deep into his mouth? How many times had he thought about holding her? Kissing her? Bending her over a chair and taking her until her eyes rolled back in her head and his balls burst from the pleasure?

As if on cue, Natalie reached between them and cupped him through his jeans. He jerked hard against her and felt his breath leave him in a startled whoosh.

"You're trying to kill me, aren't you?" he choked out, pushing against her clever palm.

She found the snap, then the zipper whined as she pulled it down. "Killing you would hardly serve my purposes." She wrapped her hand around him and stroked. "I need you both *stiff* and *alive*."

Rough laughter erupted from his throat. He'd been around her long enough to know that she had an outrageous sense of humor. He just wasn't used to encountering it under these particular circumstances—her hand down his pants, working his dick with enough skill to have him prepared for launch and ready to detonate at any second.

He needed to distract her, Levi thought, or he didn't have a prayer in hell of holding it together. In fact, a few more strokes and he was going to lose it.

Not like this, dammit. When he came, he fully intended to be inside her.

Time to turn the tables.

Reaching down, he eased his hand beneath her dress and made a determined trek up the inside of her thigh. He found a ridiculously small triangle of silky fabric over her curls and smiled against her lips when he realized it was gratifyingly damp. She squirmed against his fingers and made a little mewling sound in her throat.

Predictably—thankfully—her hand stilled against him.

He rubbed her, wishing that he'd had the fore-thought to bring a condom. But, sleeping with her tonight hadn't been in his plans. Tonight he'd planned to move in and test the waters.

What he hadn't expected was losing any pretense of control.

He should have, but he hadn't. Furthermore, there was a reason he'd wanted to wait, though for the life of him right now he couldn't remember it. Something about fulfilling her fantasies, but at the moment, all he wanted to do was fill her. With himself.

Right here against her front door. Hadn't that been one of her fantasies? Levi thought as he backed her up and slipped a finger between her nether lips. He unerringly found the little nub at the top of her sex and thumbed it, drawing a broken breath from her chest.

"You don't play fair."

"Fair's for pansies," Levi said, dipping a finger inside, then coating her with her own juices. He felt a single bead of moisture leak from his dick and a sweat broke out across his forehead.

Man, how he wanted her.

To hell with plans. To hell with everything.

He kissed a path down her throat, then licked one over the top of her breast and watched the nipple pucker for him. Pouting nipples, hot sex...

Doomed. Utterly doomed.

"Natalie, I didn't—I don't have any protection. You wouldn't happen to—"

"What?" she asked, her voice tortured as she worked herself against him, hovering on what he knew was the edge of climax. The straps on her sundress sagged, revealing her cleavage. "You didn't bring anything?"

"No," he admitted. She clamped herself around him, her greedy sex clutching his fingers. So damned responsive, he thought. And so very, very close. He hooked one finger inside and angled up, then knuckled her clit harder.

Her mouth opened in a silent scream and seconds later she spasmed hard around him. Her breathing came in labored little puffs and she clung to him, seemingly unable to stand.

A moment later, a satisfied smile curled her lips

as she looked up at him. "Then the next time you come to my door you need to take a lesson from the Boy Scouts," Natalie told him. "And *be prepared*."

Another laugh rattled out of his chest. "Duly noted."

He pressed another kiss to her lips.

Make no mistake—he would be.

9

Dear Levi,
Do you remember the time you sacked that guy on the beach for hitting his girlfriend? Did you know that's the moment you melted my heart? Did you know that's the instant I fell in love with you?

"I can't believe you didn't just tell him you were the one who's been writing the letters," Winnie admonished, exasperated. "I don't understand what the big deal is now. I could see it before—the possibility of humiliation and all—but now?" She shook her head, looking as though she'd like to shake Natalie instead. "I just don't get it. He *likes* you, you little neurotic moron. *Tell him.*"

Thankful that the bakery was empty and that no one was privy to Winnie's unusually loud advice, Natalie popped a bite of iced sugar cookie into her mouth and nodded. "I will. Really."

"When?" her friend pressed.

"Today." Natalie's cheeks puffed as she exhaled mightily. "If the letter does come today, then I'll tell him."

"If you don't, then I will," Winnie threatened.

Natalie felt her eyes widen, certain that her friend had to be joking. "You wouldn't," she breathed, slightly horrified. What the hell was wrong with Winnie? She'd been a bit out of sorts since Natalie had come in a few minutes ago.

Winnie rolled her eyes. "Of course, I wouldn't. I just hate to see you blow this."

Marginally mollified, Natalie leaned against the counter. "I'm not blowing it. Didn't you hear anything I said? He told me that he'd wanted to kiss me for years, that the only reason he'd never made a play for me was because he thought that Adam and I might eventually become a thing."

Winnie's eyes widened significantly and she snorted. "Him and everybody else," she said.

Ah, Natalie realized. Now they were getting somewhere. *Adam.* "How did seeing Adam go the other day?"

Winnie immediately busied herself wiping down a display case. "Fine."

"He said you'd come by."

"I took your advice and fixed him a care package." Natalie watched her closely. "Yeah?"

Winnie's face crumpled in frustration. "I'd have been better off if I'd been a petit four," she all but wailed. "Oh, Natalie, I just need to forget him. I need to move on, to let it go…and yet I can't. I've tried."

"What happened?"

She smiled sadly. "Nothing. That's just it. He barely looked at me and had less to say."

Natalie frowned. "He was unfriendly?" That didn't sound like Adam.

"Not unfriendly. Just…uninterested. I mentioned coaching my softball team—something he would have been interested in before—but he only grunted. I told him about training for that 10K I'm running in the fall and he muttered a weak congratulations." Her small shoulders lifted in a fatalistic shrug. "I wish I'd never gone over there. Seeing him was hard enough. Seeing him and realizing that he can't even drum up the enthusiasm to make small talk with me? That's worse."

Natalie tsked under her breath. "Winnie, I'm sorry. I don't know what to say. Adam's just been Adam with me, you know? I just assumed—"

Winnie's lips twisted with bitter humor and her blue eyes glazed with unshed tears. "He's always been 'just Adam' with you, Nat. You have no idea how much I envy you that."

"Oh, Winnie," Natalie said, her voice thick as she pulled her friend into a hug. "I'm so sorry. I wish I knew—"

The bell tinkled over the door, interrupting what she was about to say, and Adam's low whistle filled in the rest of her sentence. "Damn. If I'd known I was going to get to see a little girl-on-girl action along with one of the best cookies in the world, I would have been coming down here every morning."

Winnie's wide-eyed gaze swung to Adam and she blinked, then quickly dashed away the lone tear that had escaped.

Naturally, Adam didn't miss it. He looked questioningly at Natalie and she aimed an I'll-deal-with-you-later look in his direction.

He merely blinked innocently. "I've been looking for you," he told her. "I went by the gallery first, but when you weren't there I figured I'd find you here."

Winnie turned away and pretended to check on the éclair case.

Torn between both friends, Natalie crossed her arms over her chest. "Why have you been looking for me?"

"Because I can't get anything out of my tight-lipped brother and wanted to know how things went last night."

Natalie pressed her lips together to keep from smiling. "Things went fine. He liked my lasagna."

Adam stared at her. "That's it? I practically shove the two of you together, spend a lonely night at home in front of the television when I could have been watching a miserable chick flick with you, and *that's* all you're going to give me? 'He liked my lasagna'?"

Natalie shrugged, enjoying this more than she should. "'Fraid so."

Adam swung his outraged gaze to Winnie, evidently hoping that she would give him the scoop. Winnie merely grinned. "It's damn good lasagna." She grinned back and forth between the two of them. "But I will tell you this—"

Natalie whirled on her friend.

"—they *didn't* watch a chick flick."

"Winnie!" she admonished, outraged.

A wide grin split Adam's face and he turned to stare at her. "Well, well, well. If you didn't watch a movie, just what did you do?"

"She didn't say that we didn't watch a movie," Natalie objected. "She said we didn't watch a chick flick."

Adam chewed the inside of his cheek. "What did you watch?"

"I'll never tell," Natalie said, because she knew it would infuriate him.

He looked to Winnie, and Natalie silently willed her friend to be strong. "Well?"

"They watched *The Shining*."

Stunned at how quickly her friend had caved, Natalie felt her mouth drop open. "I can't believe you just did that."

"You've got too many secrets," Winnie said archly.

"Not anymore," Adam remarked, staring across the street at the post office. A smug grin she absolutely didn't trust curled his lips. "Levi's got a handful of mail and he's wearing a smile so big I can count his teeth from here. Oh, and look. He's headed toward your gallery." To Natalie's absolute shock, Adam poked his head out the door and bellowed at his brother. "Hey! She's down here!" He rubbed his hands together, then hobbled over to a chair and sat down. "In the absence of popcorn, I'll have one of those little cake thingies. Come join me, Winnie. We're about to have ringside seats."

Natalie gaped at them.

Adam tsked and shook his head. "I can count your teeth, too, but obviously for different reasons."

"Asshole," Natalie said. "Would you shut up?"

"You were going to tell him today anyway," Winnie pointed out.

The sugar cookie she'd eaten only moments before churned in her belly and she resisted the pressing urge to flee from the store. This had been coming. She'd known it. She'd known the letter was going to get here. She'd known he was going to find out that she'd been the one writing him.

She'd known it…and yet she wasn't prepared.

Two seconds later, Levi appeared at the door. The look in his eyes—hot and happy and confused— slammed into her before he entered the store.

She saw the envelope in his hand, recognized her address stamp from where she stood. Nausea hit and, hand over her mouth, she bolted to the bathroom.

Five minutes later, after brushing her teeth—she always carried a toothbrush and paste for this very reason—Natalie steeled herself for what was to come and opened the door.

Levi stood there, leaning against the wall in the small hallway, away from the main dining room. He looked up from the letter in his hand.

"You've got to quit doing this," he said, jerking his head toward the bathroom. "This is not the kind of thing a guy wants to inspire in a woman."

Natalie crossed her arms over her chest and rubbed the back of her calf with her foot. She gestured toward the letter. "You know perfectly well how you inspire me," she said. "Especially now."

Levi waited until her eyes met his. "I don't understand. You put a return address on this one. Why couldn't you just tell me? I all but asked you last night."

Natalie looked away, feeling a flush creep up her neck. "Er…the thing is…*I* didn't exactly stamp the return address on it."

A line emerged between his brows and an unsure smile curved his lips. "I'm not following."

"It's okay," she said. "You can't always know everything."

"Natalie."

"Lacey, my assistant, did it," she admitted, releasing a pent-up breath. "In a rare instance of efficiency, she noticed the letter on my desk, stamped it and took it to the post office along with my other promotional mailings."

A slow grin slid over Levi's lips. "You mean this was an accident?"

She nodded and lowered her head. "Of epic proportions. You were never supposed to know it was me."

"Never?"

"At least not until I was ready to tell you."

Levi moved forward, put a finger underneath her chin and lifted it up slightly. "Would you ever have told me?"

"I was going to tell you today. You can ask Winnie. That's what we were just talking about."

"You could have told me this morning," he pointed out. "When we were combing."

Too true, she knew. She was such a coward. "That wasn't the right time."

He chuckled softly and she felt that wicked laugh in her belly. "Why not?"

"Because I was thinking about other things."

"Like what?"

"Like what I'd written in those letters." Like

kissing him, and rolling around in the sand with him, and feeling his wonderful bare ass beneath her hands, and the hardest part of him pushing in and out of the softest part of her. She'd been thinking about licking him from one end to the other and savoring the smell of him and wrapping her legs around his waist.

Levi's gaze darkened. "You mean like how much you want me?"

She gave an embarrassed chuckle. "I think we've pretty much established that."

"Do you remember what I told you last night?" he asked, sidling closer to her.

Her gaze searched his. "A-about what?"

He backed her against the wall and planted a hand on either side of her head. He was about to lay siege again, Natalie realized, and he was bringing the heavy artillery. "About not wasting any more time."

"Oh, yeah."

"Want me to tell you where I went before I dropped by the post office?"

He nuzzled her neck and her breath hitched in her lungs. Longing knifed through her and heat slickened her folds. Her nipples pearled beneath the thin fabric of her bra. "Wh-where?"

"The drug store. I might not be a Boy Scout, but baby, I'm prepared."

LEVI STARTED to back her into the bathroom, but Natalie retained just enough sense to halt him. "Not in there," she said between kisses. She'd just tossed her cookies—literally—in there. "Here," she said, dragging him toward Winnie's storeroom.

She looped her arms around his neck and, with a little jump, wrapped her legs around his waist. Levi determinedly pushed inside the small, darkened room, then closed the door with his foot.

"Lock it," she mumbled against his mouth.

"They're not coming in. I told them we'd need some privacy."

Natalie chuckled, suckling his bottom lip. "Sounds like you thought of everything."

Levi kissed her until every bone in her body felt as though it had melted. He dragged her shirt up over her head and tugged the strings of her bikini top loose with his teeth. He growled low in his throat. "Do you have any idea how many times I've dreamed of doing that? This damned bikini drives me nuts. *You* drive me nuts."

Pleasure bloomed in her chest as she dragged his shirt from the waistband of his jeans. "You've always had a pretty depraved effect on me, too. As you well know."

"Wanna know a secret?"

"You know all of mine," she pointed out. "I think knowing *one* of yours is only fair."

Levi drew back and his heavy-lidded gaze met hers. She saw desire and need and something else…something more elemental and altogether dangerous. "I wanted it to be you. I would lie there at night in the barracks and picture you doing the things to me that you'd written. It was *your* face I saw when I read your letters. It was you I wrote back to." He released a shaky breath. "It was you, Nat, all along."

"Oh, Levi," she said, her heart in her throat. He had no idea how much that meant to her. How deeply that "secret" he'd just shared affected her. She felt the backs of her eyes tingle.

Levi kissed one lid and then the other, then his mouth slipped lower until it covered her own. His lips brushed hers once, twice, and then it was as though something snapped between them. The tentative grasp on control gave way and suddenly he was kissing her until she thought she couldn't breathe and ultimately, didn't want to if it meant he'd stop.

Clothes vanished—her bikini top, his shirt, her shorts, his jeans. Her bikini bottom and his boxers later, they were rolling around on the floor of Winnie's pantry—bits of flour and sugar everywhere—completely naked and completely, totally happy. She landed on top.

Levi bent forward, pulled her nipple into his mouth and suckled her. "Damn, you taste good."

"Not as good as you feel," Natalie told him,

smiling at the sugar smudge on his cheek. She leaned down and licked it off, then purposely settled her sex over the hot ridge of his arousal.

Hot, hard and huge. Her lids fluttered shut as sweet sensation bolted through her.

She couldn't believe this was finally happening. After all these years, all of her pining for him, her letters…he was finally going to be hers.

And it couldn't happen soon enough.

She didn't want slow and easy—they'd have time for that later.

She wanted him *now*. "Prepare yourself," she said, widening her eyes meaningfully.

Levi laughed, but did as she instructed, smoothing the protection into place. A second later, Natalie hovered above him, then sank slowly onto the long, hard length of him. The air left her lungs in a soft hiss as she seated herself firmly onto him.

Levi's fingers dug into her hips and he bared his teeth in a feral sort of smile that was strangely sexy. Their eyes locked, and in that moment, everything inside of her seemed to click into place. She looked into his eyes and saw her future children, her happiness, her very world. This was happening here and now for a reason, Natalie realized as she bent forward and licked a flat, masculine nipple.

Levi flexed beneath her, pushing deeper. His hands slid around and shaped her rump, almost possessively, and the sensation was nothing short of amazing. He was hot and hard, soft skin and lean muscle and, for the moment, completely, utterly hers.

And that thought simply did it for her.

Natalie leaned back and worked herself up and down the length of him. Her clit tingled and her breasts grew heavy and her neck suddenly didn't feel as if it could support her head, but none of that mattered because she was close, so very close to—

Levi upped the tempo beneath her, bucking deliberately. He bent forward and took the crown of her breast into his hot mouth and laved her nipple with his tongue. He palmed her other breast, abrading the sensitive peak, rolling it between his thumb and forefinger.

Little sparklers started dancing behind her closed lids and her belly grew impossibly hot and muddled. The first flash of impending climax quickened in her womb and she felt Levi harden even more inside of her.

She rode him harder, up and down, up and down, pushing, reaching, desperate for the release she'd waited so very long for.

"Levi, I need—"

"Me," he said, going deeper, holding her hips as he took over and pistoned in and out of her. "You need *me*."

Oh, yes, Natalie thought. She did. She needed

him. Loved him. Had always loved him. This was what she'd been waiting for. *Him. Inside her.*

Harder and faster and harder still, he kept on, pushing into her heat, pummeling her sex, nailing her swollen clit with each relentless thrust.

He pushed again, one, two times, three, then squeezed her rear, and she literally came so hard her back felt as if it would break from the impact.

She stiffened above him, her mouth opened and a long, keening cry, ripped from her very soul, tore from her throat. Levi bent forward and caught that scream of release with his mouth, ate it and savored it. She felt him pulsing deep inside of her, then he suddenly went rigid and joined her in the wonderful world of Orgasm Land.

Breathing hard, Natalie collapsed on top of him. She could feel his heart pounding beneath her chest and there was something so affirming about that steady thump-thump-thump that tears inexplicably burned in her eyes.

At last. And it was everything she'd ever dreamed of and more. So much more.

His long, talented fingers stroked down her back, then up again, and tangled in her hair. She could feel him testing the strands against his fingers, curling the length of them around his hand.

"This makes me want to drag you back to my cave and never let you go."

Natalie grinned and kissed his chest, then gave her feminine muscles a gentle squeeze. "This makes me want to let you."

"That was amazing," he said, his voice a bit rusty.

"I won't be lodging a complaint."

His breathing slowed and he continued to play with her hair. "Do you have plans for tonight?"

She drew a half-heart on his side. "Not until you ask me to do something."

His chuckle made her cheek vibrate. "Come out on the boat with me," he said softly. "Me, you and the moonlight. What do you say?"

Yes, yes, yes. "So long as you're *prepared,* I'm there."

Levi's laugh stirred her hair and that sexy chuckle settled warmly around her heart. "You bet."

10

Dear Levi,
This morning I woke up and my first thought
was of you. I imagined your naked body
twisted in my sheets and your head resting
against my rumpled pillow…

LEVI TOOK Natalie's hand as she climbed aboard the
boat. "Did you tell your dad we were doing this?"

As though it were the most natural thing in the
world, Natalie leaned forward and pressed a kiss
against his cheek. "Of course not. He would just
worry."

"Natalie." He didn't think anything would go
wrong, but he hated the idea of keeping her father out
of the loop.

"I've brought my cell phone," Natalie told him. "If
he calls me and asks where I am, then I won't lie. I'll
tell him the truth."

Fair enough, he supposed. Still, John really needed
to face this obsessive fear. He and Natalie lived in a

bayside community, a stone's throw from the Atlantic. She worked in and around the shore all the time. He was going to have to give her some room; otherwise Levi could see a problem developing.

"How's your uncle Milton?"

"He's doing better," Natalie said, settling onto a bench seat. She dropped her bag at her feet—he'd told her to plan on spending the night—and had the pleasure of watching a beautiful smile move over her raspberry lips as he pulled away from the dock. "And it's been good for Dad to be there, too. He and Uncle Milton have been playing chess and watching Andy Griffith reruns. He needs other interests besides—" She frowned, seemingly struggling to find the right word.

"You," Levi supplied.

She grinned. "That works, yes."

Truth be told, he could hardly fault her father. He seriously suspected that, given the time, his interest would be solely focused on her as well. He could easily see his world narrowing down until only she was in view, until all he could think about was the shape of her smile, the sound of her laugh, the achingly beautiful curve of her cheek, those adorable freckles on her small nose, the way her long hair naturally curved to the shape of her pert little face.

And then there were the other things... The things that made him go hard.

The exact shade of her dusky nipples—a deep rosy hue. The gentle swell of her naked hip, the ripe feel of her wonderful ass in his hands. The way her dark-brown eyes went all soft and heavy-lidded when he was inside her.

Today had been…beyond his wildest dreams.

Getting the letter had been nice, having his suspicions confirmed a perk. But taking her in Winnie's storeroom had been, hands-down, the best thing that had ever happened to him.

Reading her letters, Levi had known that she wanted him. That she literally ached for him. But having all that passion, the complete surrender of any reservation, manifest itself in his arms… Sweet Lord.

He was ruined, Levi thought.

He'd never—*never*—known sex could be anything like what they'd experienced. They hadn't just made love or merely had sex—they'd connected on a level beyond anything he could have ever imagined. They'd *exploded* together.

Just looking at her right now made him go hard. His fingers actually shook on the wheel and it was all he could do not to drop anchor and drag her down to his little bedroom.

And he would. In due time.

Until then, he wanted to recreate one of her fantasies. She'd once told him that she wanted to make it on his boat, to feel him rocking above her as the boat rocked below.

He was *so* willing to accommodate.

Despite the fact that time was so very short, Levi had every intention of fulfilling each and every fantasy that she'd written to him. For this single moment in time, he had the ability to make her dreams come true and, though he couldn't offer her forever, he could offer her right now.

"How's Adam doing?" Natalie asked. "Winnie mentioned that he'd been distant when she'd visited yesterday."

Levi settled in behind the wheel. "He's going stir crazy," he said. "He's not healing as quickly as he'd like to and that's frustrating. Then there's the emotional trauma he claims doesn't exist, but I know better. He's lost part of his leg. He's in mourning for that, whether he'll admit it or not."

Levi couldn't begin to imagine what his brother was going through. Though he knew Adam would eventually do everything he set his mind to, Levi didn't think he'd factored in sufficient time for the recovery period.

"As for Winnie." Levi made a face. "They've always had a very competitive relationship and he's respected that about her. He's probably worried about losing face. And…she's always had a thing for him, right?"

Natalie nodded. "I knew that Adam was aware of it, but not you."

"We're brothers," he said by way of explanation.

"Anyway, if I were in his shoes, I'd be worried about no longer holding her interest, if you catch my drift."

Natalie's eyes widened. "You mean because of the accident?"

"Exactly."

"That's absurd."

He smiled and shook his head. "That's a man."

Natalie grew thoughtful for a moment, and he watched her worry her bottom lip. "Winnie would never be so shallow. She hates what happened, Levi—we all do." She shook her head. "But she's in love with him. Her feelings aren't going to change because he's lost part of his leg. He's the one who keeps insisting that he's the same person. He can't play it both ways. He's either the same or he isn't."

Levi chuckled. "Have fun telling him that."

She nodded pertly. "I will."

Levi aimed the boat out toward the middle of the bay and felt the familiar peace that always settled around him whenever he was on the water. The sun was sinking low on the horizon, painting the ocean in various shades of shimmering blue, pink and orange. Without warning, Natalie's arms came around his waist and she rested her cheek on his back. Something in his chest tightened and expanded, making it momentarily hard to breathe.

"It's beautiful, isn't it?" she said, sighing contentedly.

Though he'd been on many different bodies of

water, Bethel Bay would always be the standard by which he judged them. He tugged her around and slung an arm over her shoulder, feeling more content than he could ever remember. "It is."

"I love Bethel Bay. It's got everything, you know? It's small enough to know most everyone, but big enough to have a little culture. And the view." She gestured to the shoreline and the vast expanse of blue water. "Second to none."

They were treading into dangerous territory and he knew it.

Natalie drew back so that she could look at him. Excitement glittered in her eyes. "You should come to my walking tour Friday night."

"What?"

"I do a walking tour of the downtown area every Friday night. Go over the history of the town. Talk about the rum runners and the smugglers who used to frequent our little burg. It's quite fascinating."

Seems like he remembered Adam saying something about that. Come to think of it, maybe Adam would like to go. One of the things his physical therapist had mentioned was getting more exercise. "Would you mind if I brought Adam along?"

"Absolutely not." A concerned line wrinkled her brow. "Are you sure that it wouldn't be too much for him?"

Levi related what the physical therapist had said.

"He's got the temporary prosthesis. He needs to move."

"Then bring him." Her gaze locked on his. "And I was kind of hoping you could come to my place and spend the night. It's selfish, I know, but…"

"I'd planned on inviting myself over," Levi admitted as a rush of pleasure skittered through his chest. He gave her a little squeeze. "You can be selfish with me anytime."

A shadow darkened her eyes. "Not true," she said. "You leave Saturday, right?"

He knew they needed to talk about this, but that didn't make it any easier. He didn't want to talk about leaving her when he'd just found her. But at the same time, he had a job to do. Being a Ranger— it was who he was. He was part of a team—a brotherhood of men who were committed to doing things for the greater good. He couldn't just change that…even if he were tempted. And God help him, he was. "I do."

"What time?"

"I fly out at nine, but will need to leave the house no later than six." He swallowed. "You know how that goes."

"So we'll need to say our goodbyes Friday night, then."

He nodded. "I'm afraid so. Unless you want to ride to—"

She shook her head. "No, I don't think so," she admitted shakily. "That's, uh— That's family time."

He understood. Speaking of family, his had certainly celebrated the fact he was seeing Natalie. His brother had wasted no time in telling his mother, who'd happily given her blessing. "She's a lovely girl, your Natalie," she'd told him, smiling with approval.

Your Natalie. Those two little words had affected him more than he would have ever imagined. She *was* his. How in the world was he going to leave her?

Time to change the subject, to talk about something more pleasant. Like his plans for the evening. "Are you getting hungry?"

She looked up, her eyes inviting. She was hungry, all right, but not for food. "I could eat." She paused. "You."

The perpetual hard-on he'd been experiencing hit critical level. Levi chuckled softly under his breath, then bent and kissed her lips. "I'm *definitely* on the menu."

"Then I plan to get full."

NATALIE WAITED for Levi to drop anchor, then threaded her fingers through his and tugged him toward the small bedroom. Talking about him leaving had only emphasized the fact that she had very little time left to spend with Levi. And she'd be damned if she'd waste that time with if-onlys and what-might-have-beens. She knew the score going into this very brief relationship and, rather than dwell on what she couldn't change, she planned to take advantage of every second they had left.

Beginning now.

Her fantasy lover—the bona fide love of her life—was standing right here in front of her, ready to do her bidding, ready to make her dreams come true, ready to rock her world.

And she looked forward to the quake.

This morning she'd been so desperate, in such a hurry to get him beneath her skin that she hadn't been able to give much thought to anything else. Frankly, she'd just needed to take the edge off.

And while this morning's frantic sex session in Winnie's storeroom—she was still finding the occasional grain of sugar on her body—had done just that, it had also done something more.

It had whetted her appetite.

She hadn't been kidding when she said she wanted to eat him. She did. She wanted to taste the hot, hard length of him. She wanted to feel that silky skin against her tongue. She wanted to suck him up like an ice-cream cone on the Fourth of July, then set him off like a Roman candle.

Natalie shrugged out of her shirt, then shucked her pants. "You're going to need to get naked for this."

Levi's hungry gaze slid from one end of her body to the other in a slow leisurely process that set her blood on fire and made her nipples bud. He instantly stripped, then lay down on the bed and linked his hands casually behind his head. "Done."

Natalie deliberately popped the front closure on her bra and let it fall open, then casually shrugged out of it. Next, she slowly shimmied out of her panties—although there hadn't been much to them—and kicked them aside.

A stuttering breath echoed out of his lungs. *"Wow."*

Pleased, she set one knee against the bed, then trailed her hand slowly up over his thigh. His penis jumped, almost as if it were trying to land in her hand. She feasted her eyes on him, on the part of him that was so very different from her. He was hard and hot and the slippery skin glided effortlessly against her palm as she explored him.

His breath hissed through his clenched teeth. "Natalie," he said warningly.

She bent and touched her tongue to the very tip.

He swore.

"Yes?" she asked.

"You're doing this on purpose."

She took the whole of him in her mouth and sucked long and hard. "I thought that was the whole point."

"I'm going to get you back for this," he promised, his voice cracking. "I am *so* going to get you back. You're not the only one who's hungry."

She quirked a brow at him. "Who says we have to dine alone?"

His head popped off the pillow, his eyes widened, and then a long, slow smile designed to set her panties—had she been wearing any—on fire slid over his beautiful lips. "You're right. We don't."

Before she knew what was happening, Levi took hold of her legs and dragged her into position. His fingers parted her curls and a second later, his hot tongue was fastened over the heart of her sex, licking and sucking.

Pleasure bolted through her and she transferred her joy to him, cupping his balls, sucking the whole of him into her mouth once more. She nibbled, she licked. She wrapped her hand around his dick and chased it with her lips, up and down the long shaft. Meanwhile he continued his own frenzied assault, tenting his tongue over her engorged clit and rubbing hard against her. He hooked a finger deep inside her wet channel, finding the sensitive patch of skin she'd only ever read about.

Natalie sucked him harder, could feel the climax building in his balls as they shrunk up and hardened.

"Natalie, you'd better stop," he said, his voice strangled.

"Only if you will," she challenged.

Levi snagged a condom—one of many he'd put on the small nightstand—and tore into the package with his teeth before fishing it out.

Natalie took it from him. "Let me," she said, carefully rolling the protection into place. "And for the record, I'm on the pill and I've got a clean bill of health."

Levi flipped her over and nudged her folds, bumping the top of her sex. Her eyes rolled back in her head. "For the record, I don't need to be on the pill, and I also have a clean bill of health." He flashed his teeth in a smile. "But I was prepared."

Natalie chuckled, then the laugh died a swift death as he suddenly pushed into her. Veins stood out on his neck and his entire body quivered atop her. *He's so beautiful,* Natalie thought as her body welcomed him inside. She drew her legs back and wrapped them around his waist, rocking against him. He was absolutely amazing. From an artist's viewpoint, utterly flawless. A beautiful creation of muscle and bone, and those eyes… They had the ability to look right into her soul.

"Damn," he muttered.

He withdrew almost to the tip, then pushed back in. "I know."

Levi bent and nuzzled her neck, then licked a path between her breasts and over one sensitive aching peak. She felt that sensation all the way to the heart of her sex, as though an invisible thread connected the two. She tightened around him, holding him in, and ran her hands along his back, then around and up and over his chest. She loved the way he felt, Natalie thought, as her greedy palms devoured him. Soft yet hard, unapologetically male. He was certainly no metrosexual. She'd bet her life that he'd never had a manicure and wouldn't know a male moisturizer if it bit him on the ass.

He was a man. Every wonderfully proportioned divine inch of him.

Levi paused, looking adorably uncertain. "Do I want to know what you're thinking?"

She grinned up at him and flexed her hips, rocking forward. "I think you're hot."

He pushed again. "Good. I like it when you think I'm hot."

"And I was thinking that I'm glad that you're not a metrosexual—"

"A *what?*"

"—and that you've never had a manicure and that you don't moisturize before bed."

Levi peered down at her. "You know what I'm thinking?"

"No."

"I'm thinking that if you're thinking that much, I must not be doing this right." He banded his arm around her waist, hiked her leg higher and angled deep. "Time to rectify."

And he did.

Oh, sweet heaven help me, Natalie thought as he pounded into her. Hot, long, relentless strokes, deeper and deeper. She wrapped her legs tighter around him and met him thrust for thrust, though it was hard to keep up.

In and out, in and out, he pushed her higher and higher until she could feel the burn of climax hovering in her womb, just a bit out of reach, but growing closer with every powerful thrust.

"Levi, I—" She couldn't finish, couldn't form another word, but he seemed to know what she needed because at that precise moment he reached down between their joined bodies and thumbed her clit.

She came.

The orgasm washed through her like a giant pulsating wave, lifting her up, pulling her under, drowning her in pleasure. Just when she'd reached the surface and was content to float along the languid river of release, Levi suddenly flipped her over onto her belly, dragged her hips up against him, and pushed into her from behind.

Unbelievably, pleasure bolted through her. He plowed into her, over and over, his balls slapping against her aching flesh. It was a good thing he was holding her up, Natalie thought, because there was no way in hell she could support her own weight. Her entire body felt boneless, and another tingle of unexpected release quickened deep inside of her.

It was almost as if he knew it, too, as though he had some sort of psychic connection to her sex, because he angled up and pushed harder, reaching for that place that would set her off once more.

Harder, deeper and deeper still…

Her breath came in short little puffs and her vision

blackened around the edges. She didn't believe it was possible to die from pleasure, but was seriously beginning to wonder if that was what was happening to her. Her heart was pounding so hard she couldn't catch her breath. Her heavy, sensitive breasts bounced back and forth on her chest, absorbing the force of his thrusts.

"Come for me again, Nat," he said, licking a path up the middle of her back. He nipped at her shoulder, sending her over the edge of release again. She spasmed around him, and another contraction of almost unbearable sensation eddied through her.

Her climax triggered his own. She felt him stiffen behind her, and he angled deep, seating himself as deeply into her as he could. Warmth pooled in the end of the condom, setting off another little pulse of release.

A moment later, he snagged a tissue from the table and disposed of the protection, then cuddled her close. She could hear the waves lapping against the side of the boat, and saw that the first twinkle of stars had appeared. A half moon glowed overhead, and for that instant, everything was completely, totally right with her world.

Because she was in love with Levi McPherson.

11

Dear Levi,
Sometimes when I can't sleep, I pretend that you can't either, and that you're awake in your bed, thinking of me, too. I pretend that you love me and want me as much as I want you…

"THIS IS excellent," Natalie said, slicing off another bite of her steak.

"It's kind of hard to ruin a good piece of meat," Levi said, trying not to let her appreciation go to his head. It had been a while since he'd cooked for a woman, but he still knew how to work a grill. He'd picked up a couple of steaks in town as well as some fresh ears of corn and had tossed both on the fire. The German potato salad he'd asked his mother to fix for him and the dessert that Winnie had thrown in completed the meal.

Or their *second* one, anyway.

Sex had a way of making him hungry, and the great sex he'd just had made him absolutely ravenous.

His gaze slid over Natalie, who'd shrugged into one of his shirts. The army-green T-shirt hit her mid-thigh as she sat cross-legged in the chair, her long red hair sliding in a tangled mass over her right shoulder.

Gorgeous, Levi thought, and his throat went strangely tight. He didn't know when he'd ever felt so strongly about a woman, when he'd ever felt more alive and connected and at ease with one. Natalie had a way of doing that. He could enjoy dinner with her, walk along the beach with her—hell, just watch her breathe—and knew he'd never tire of her. He knew that she'd always feel like a comfortable old pair of shoes, easy to slip into. His lips curved. Not that she would appreciate the analogy, but he'd never been a whiz with pretty words. He just knew he cared about her. Cared about her more than he was willing to admit. More than self-preservation would let him consider.

She glanced around the bay. In the distance lights twinkled along the shore. "How long have you had this boat?"

"I got it when I graduated from jump school," Levi told her. "It was a present to myself."

She lifted her wineglass in his direction and a smile curved her ripe kiss-swollen lips. "Excellent choice," she murmured. She let go a sigh. "It's been years since I've been on the water."

Levi leaned back in his chair and stared thoughtfully into his wineglass. "I love it," he said. "I always have. There's something about getting out on the water and knowing that I'm a tiny speck on such a vast expanse. That if I set my sails in the right direction, I can go to any place in the world."

She chewed her bottom lip, staring at him as though she didn't know what to make of him. "Hidden depths," she said. "That was a very interesting insight."

Levi chuckled, suddenly embarrassed. "I don't know about that. I just like sailing. I love the scent of the ocean and the snap of the sails. Harnessing the wind." He leaned forward. "Have you ever really thought about those early explorers? The courage it must have taken to set sail for parts unknown?"

Her eyes twinkled. "As a matter of fact, I have," she confided. "Of course, if it had all been left up to me, then we'd still be laboring under the assumption that the world was flat." She shook her head. "I wouldn't have had the courage. But you would, wouldn't you?" She nodded and rested her chin in her hand. "You would have made one helluva explorer."

"I don't know about that," Levi said, laughing. "But I'd like to think I would have tried. That I would have been interested."

"Is that why the military suits you so well, you think? Because of all the travel? Of going to parts unknown?"

He nodded thoughtfully. He'd never really considered that aspect of it before, but he supposed that was part of the lure. That and defending and protecting his country. He had a healthy respect for the men who'd essentially risked treason to found this country. They were men of courage, of character. He liked to believe that he was contributing to their cause, that he was playing a small part in their plan.

"I suppose," he finally admitted. "I love seeing new places and learning new customs. I've stood at the base of the Pyramids of Giza, walked part of the Great Wall of China. I've breathed highland air in Scotland and swum along the Great Barrier Reef in Australia." He smiled at her. "And I'm not done yet. There's so much more of this world that I want to see, Natalie." He paused and watched her glass stall at her lips. "You'd love it, too."

She nodded, but a sadness tinged her gaze. "I would," she agreed. "But when I was done with all that, I'd want to come home to Bethel Bay. I want to make a difference, too, Levi," she said. "I'm just doing it at a local level. And I suspect that's never going to be enough for you."

She was right, he knew, and yet hearing her say it was much harder than he'd anticipated. "Where does that leave us, then?" He asked the question lightly, as if her answer didn't really matter.

But it did.

She shrugged sadly, and he watched her swallow

before a weak smile finally managed to curl her lips. "It leaves us with tonight and tomorrow and tomorrow night…and our letters."

His gaze slammed into hers and held. "That's not enough."

"Unfortunately it has to be, doesn't it?"

"My tour is up in two months," he said.

"And then you'll just get reassigned to some other part of the world, won't you? I mean, that's been the norm, right?"

"It has," he admitted.

Natalie reached across the table and took his hand. "I knew this when we started, Levi. In fact, having any part of you at all is more than I ever expected."

"Then your expectations were too low."

"Maybe so, but I didn't know you were interested in me. You always hid it so well."

A droll smile caught his lips. "Hi, pot. Meet kettle."

She chuckled, and that wonderfully feminine sound wrapped around his middle and squeezed. "I know," she said. "But you have to understand. I never in a million years dreamed that I'd get to be with you at all. Do I wish we had time for more? Yes. Am I expecting anything more than what we have right now?" She shook her head. "No. And I can be okay with that. I have to be. Because you're not coming back here and I'm not leaving. I can't.

My father is here, my business is here." She shrugged. "It is what it is...and I'm loving every minute of it."

He grimly suspected he was loving her, Levi thought, stunned that this had somehow happened. He'd known that he'd always been drawn to her, intrigued by her. But in love? *In love?*

Unfortunately, he knew she was right. This was a problem that had no answer. She was too invested in Bethel Bay and he was too invested in his career. He could no more change than she could, and he'd be damned before he'd ask her. Things would probably be fine for a little while, but eventually she'd begin to hate him for taking her away from home. Were he to make the same sacrifice for her, no doubt that same logic would hold true.

It was a no-win situation.

He'd known that going in, had even made sure she understood the rules before they started, and yet here he was trying to figure out a way around the policy.

Evidently deciding that a subject change was in order, Natalie let go a sigh, and a smile that wasn't altogether true slid over her lips. "So now that you've painted over the *Sabrina,* what are you going to christen your boat?"

Levi laughed. "I have no idea. I'm just glad I've gotten rid of her old moniker."

"What was she before you dubbed her the *Sabrina?*"

"The *Bitch*."

Natalie's eyes widened and she almost spewed her wine. "I'm sorry?"

He chuckled, glad that she'd found a way to lighten the moment. They only had a little time left and he'd be damned if he'd ruin it by being maudlin. "I'm joking." He thought back, trying to remember. "You know, I think it was something simple, like the *Zephyr*."

Her nose crinkled. "You can't have a boat named the *Zephyr*," Natalie said. "It doesn't suit you. It's too *Anne of Green Gables*."

Levi shrugged and refilled her empty glass. "Hey, I'm open to suggestions."

She brightened. "Really?"

He nodded.

She chewed the inside of her cheek and gazed at him with a thoughtful expression. "How about the *Badass?*"

He guffawed. "The *Badass?* I'm flattered, but I don't think so."

She sat back in her chair, seemingly deflated. "I think it has a certain ring to it."

"I'm sure you do. But it won't work. Every redneck with a boat in a hundred-mile radius will be gunning to kick my ass."

Smiling, she nodded in agreement. "I suppose you're right."

"I'll think of something," Levi said.

Natalie's sly gaze suddenly found his. "I know what you can call her," she said.

He essayed another grin and indulged her. "What?"

"Second Helping."

He frowned. "Second Hel—"

She grabbed his hand and tugged him from his chair, pressed herself suggestively against him. He hardened and instantly understood her meaning. Second helping, eh? Levi smiled down at her and kissed her. "I like the way you think."

"And I like the way you taste." She propelled him back toward the bedroom. "I'd like *my* second helping. Now."

He happily obliged. And would go back for thirds before the night was over.

"Are you sure this is a good idea?" Winnie asked, casting a furtive look over her shoulder at Adam, who was currently trailing along at the back of the group on his new temporary leg.

They were stopping for a drink at one of Bethel Bay's oldest pubs—it was the capping point of her usual tour—and Natalie sneaked a glance back at Adam. "I asked the same thing and Levi assured me that Adam's therapist said he needed the exercise."

"It makes me nervous," Winnie said.

"You need to get over it," Natalie told her. "Adam knows that you've always had a thing for him and he's worried you won't feel the same about him after the accident."

Winnie's eyes widened in outrage. "Natalie, you know that's not true. You know how I—"

"I do. But he's feeling emasculated, and the last damned thing he needs is for you to treat him any differently than you always have. He knows you care for him and he's afraid that'll change."

"It won't."

Natalie jerked her head in Adam's direction. "I'm not the one you need to convince."

Winnie nodded, seeming to mull over everything that Natalie had said. "What about you and Levi? Anything resolved on that front?"

Natalie's heart pricked. "You know nothing can be resolved. He's leaving tomorrow to go back to Iraq and I'm staying here. This is it," she said, swallowing past the sudden lump in her throat. She had to stop thinking like this, Natalie realized. She had to quit dwelling on the fact that he was about to leave and instead focus on making the most of the time they had.

Up until tonight she'd managed to do that quite well. Last night they'd spent the evening hanging out with his parents and playing cards with Adam. He'd walked her home and they'd made love on her porch swing, then talked until the sun had come up.

She'd never get tired of either, Natalie thought. Talking to him. Making love to him. Levi McPherson had always had the singular ability to make her heart sing, to engage her senses and her intellect, and he also had the rare talent of making her laugh until her sides hurt.

He…simply did it for her.

He completed her.

Or would until he left tomorrow morning, Natalie thought. And then she would curl into a ball and cry until she couldn't breathe.

Until then, she had other plans for them.

Levi and Adam sidled forward and Natalie immediately noticed the touch of confidence in the curve of Adam's smile.

"This kicks ass, Nat," he told her. "I had no idea you knew all of this stuff about Bethel Bay."

She nodded primly. "We have a unique heritage."

"This has been cool."

"Left your crutches at home, I see."

If he'd been any prouder he would have preened. "I don't need them."

"I know that's a relief."

His eyes slid to Winnie. "It beats the hell out of sitting on my ass all day, I can tell you that."

Winnie gave him a once-over. "You look like you've gained weight."

Adam gaped at her. *"What?"*

"Gained weight," she repeated. She winced at him. "I probably don't need to send any more care packages over. Now that you've got that leg, you might consider a bit of running again."

"I have not gained weight," Adam said through slightly clenched teeth.

"In fact, I lost several pounds when they lobbed off my leg."

She eyed his waistline. "Well, you seem to have found them around your middle. Maybe a few sit-ups are in order."

Natalie shared a look with Levi and it was all she could do not to burst into laughter. Winnie was definitely back to treating him the way she always had.

"Excuse me," Winnie said. "I see Mark Holbrook over there. I hear he and Susan just split up," she added in a stage whisper.

Predictably, Adam watched her walk off, and from the stunned expression on his face, it was clear he'd been blindsided by Winnie's new attitude. Glancing down at his middle, he pulled his shirt away from his body.

He quirked a brow at Levi. "Is she right? Have I gained weight? Do I look soft?"

Levi winced and considered him with a critical eye. "It wouldn't hurt to lay off the sweets and hit the gym."

Adam glared at Natalie. "Is this true? Or are they just yanking my chain?"

Knowing that Levi's motivation was to get Adam out of the house, Natalie merely shrugged regretfully. "A little exercise probably wouldn't hurt."

"Sonofabitch," Adam murmured, seemingly dumbstruck. "I'm a cow."

Natalie chuckled at him. "You're not a cow."

"Well, I sure as hell could look better." He slapped Levi on the back. "You know your way home. I'm going to the gym." He glared at Winnie, who was smiling warmly up at Mark. "Or maybe for a run."

Levi slung an arm around her shoulder and they watched Adam throw one last disgruntled look in Winnie's direction before making a determined line for the gym up the street.

"I take it you said something to Winnie."

Natalie chuckled softly and shook her head. "I sure as hell didn't tell her to tell him he looked fat."

Levi shrugged, laughing right along with her. "Hey, whatever works. Did you see the look on his face? He's been saying all week that he's determined to get back to his boys, but this is the first sign I've seen that he's actually going to do it, you know?"

"What do you think about him going back? Is it doable?"

Levi nodded slowly. "It's doable," he said. "And if he wants it bad enough, he can make it happen."

"Will he be safe?"

He blew out a breath. "Just as safe as the rest of us, I guess."

She hugged him tightly around his waist and buried her head against his upper arm. "I know I'm not supposed to say this, but you going back scares the living hell out of me."

"You can say that, Nat," Levi told her, pressing a kiss to her temple.

She looked up at him, at the achingly familiar line of his jaw. "Are you ever afraid?"

"I'd be a fool if I wasn't, wouldn't I?" He squeezed her tighter. "Adam was right. Your tour was very nice."

She nodded, pleased that he'd enjoyed it. "Thank you."

"What are we going to do now?" He pretended to be searching his memory for something important. "Seems like you mentioned doing something special for me? Am I remembering things correctly?"

The wretch. He knew damned well that she'd planned something for them. Levi had made sure that he'd recreated all of her fantasies—now it was time for her to give him one of his own.

And thanks to his most recent letter—the one that had arrived in her post-office box this morning—she had the ammunition to pull it off.

Natalie threaded her fingers through his. "Come on," she said with a significant arch of her brow. "I'm hungry."

12

Dear Levi,
I miss the sound of your laugh. It's deep and authentic and it makes me ache inside to hear it…

FIFTEEN MINUTES later, Natalie turned right onto East Bay Drive, and from Levi's vantage point in the passenger seat, it looked like they were going back to her house.

Which suited him fine.

In fact, he could honestly say that, other than being on his boat, her house had quickly become one of his favorite places in the world. It was roomy and comfortable and smacked of everything Natalie. Her scent, that sweet ginger citrus that would undoubtedly haunt his dreams, permeated the air, and he loved the lazy swirl of the ceiling fans overhead. The girl also had a healthy respect for high-end electronics, which was another sort of perk altogether.

It was hard to imagine that he'd be on a plane

tomorrow morning, headed back to Iraq by way of Fort Bragg. It didn't seem possible, Levi thought as he slid her a look. The dash lights illuminated her profile in sharp relief, emphasizing that pert little nose, elfin chin and those ripe, wonderful lips.

Something in his chest shifted, but he determinedly ignored it. He would not dwell on what he couldn't change. They'd each chosen their paths and, much as he'd like to see them come together—or hell, even intersect for more than this week—he knew it was impossible. Giving up a career he loved wasn't feasible, and convincing her to make a life with him away from Bethel Bay would, ultimately, be cruel. If he'd learned anything this week—or tonight—it was that.

Natalie loved her town and her place in it. Adam hadn't been kidding when he'd said she had a finger in nearly every pie. She was on the city council, was part of the beautification committee and a member of their Historical Society. The city and its landscape had inspired her art, for pity's sake.

She was invested.

As for his career… There had never been a time in his life when Levi had wanted to be anything other than a soldier. He was proud of what he did and who he was and, even though the idea of leaving Natalie made his gut tighten with dread, he knew he would slowly begin to dislike himself if he changed. He was a *Ranger*. And unfortunately, he didn't know how to be both a Ranger and hers.

Natalie turned into his driveway and slowly came to a stop. "Get out."

He blinked at her, surprised. "What?"

She chuckled softly. "Get out, go inside and tell your parents that you're going to bed early. You know, to rest up. And make sure you lock your bedroom door."

He felt a smile falter on his lips. He had a feeling he knew where this was going. "Should I unlock the window?"

"No."

"No?" he asked. If this was indeed his her-sneaking-into-his-bed fantasy—and he couldn't imagine what else it could be—then he knew damned well the window would need to be unlocked.

"Adam's already done it for me."

His eyes widened. "You told Adam you were going to sneak into my room through my window?"

She gave a little shrug. "I needed some inside help and didn't want to ask your parents. That would have been a bit, shall we say—" She gave a delicate shudder. "—*awkward*."

Levi cracked up, then leaned over and pressed a lingering kiss against her lips that turned into a make-out session that had him ready to drag her over into his lap and take her right there. That was a fantasy, too.

Natalie drew back. "Get inside," she said. "I'll be along shortly."

"How shortly?"

"Go," she ordered.

With another quick peck, Levi climbed from her car and made his way inside. He found his parents in the living room, sitting in front of the television watching one of their favorite game shows. They were holding hands, Levi noticed, and something about that tender display of affection wrapped around his middle and twisted.

His parents genuinely loved each other, he realized.

Naturally he'd known that. It had been evident over the years, unspoken and taken for granted. But looking at them now, sitting side by side in their matching recliners, his mother's hand in his father's... It hit him. Even after all these years—up and down and sideways, through thick and thin—*they loved each other.*

And Levi knew, if circumstances were different, that could easily be him and Natalie. He had no trouble looking into his future and seeing her by his side, holding her hand. Sharing a bed and sharing breakfast, enjoying holidays and walks on the beach.

His mother glanced up and quirked a brow. "Is something wrong, dear?"

He gave his head a gentle shake. "Nah, I'm just tired. I think I'll turn in early."

His father nodded and the rest went unsaid. Levi didn't have to say "because I have an early flight." His parents knew it. "Where's your brother?"

Levi felt a faint smile turn his lips. "He went to the gym."

A shared understanding passed between him and his father. Adam had turned a corner tonight. The General hummed under his breath, seemingly pleased. "All right then. We'll see you in the morning."

Because he knew she was putting on a brave face for his benefit, but was close to tears, Levi walked over and pressed a kiss to his mother's cheek. "G'night, Mom."

She reached up and gave him a light squeeze. "Goodnight, son."

A minute later, his heart unusually heavy, Levi closed his bedroom door behind him and locked it. He turned, and the sight that greeted him made every unpleasant thought vanish from his head.

Natalie was sprawled on her side, on his bed, *naked*.

A stunned breath stuttered out of his lungs.

Sweet mercy, she was glorious. Illuminated only by his GI Joe night-light, her body was a landscape of shadows and valleys, of glowing tanned skin and wavy red hair. A long strand slithered over her shoulder and curled provocatively around the heavy globe of her breast. If he'd ever seen anything more lovely in his life, he couldn't recall it.

It was surreal, Levi thought dimly, being in this room with her. The history of his life—Little League pictures and Uncle Sam Wants You posters, cassette tapes, his letterman jacket, various trophies and certificates…and her.

His past and present seemed to culminate completely in this moment.

She smiled then, a little uncertainly, and that small hint of vulnerability did something strange to his insides. His chest grew inexplicably tight and his throat closed, preventing speech. He couldn't have said a word if he'd wanted to.

And, he realized thankfully, he didn't have to.

Swallowing tightly, Levi walked toward the bed, shrugging out of his shirt along the way. He hit Play on the CD player and the first notes of Bob Seger's "Turn the Page" filled the air. A second later his hands were in her hair and he was feeding at her breasts. It was slow and deliberate, desperate and devastating…

Because he was in love with her.

Whether it had happened that day he'd seen her helping Adam wash his car, or when he'd received her first letter or they'd shared their first kiss—more than likely a combination of all of the above—somewhere, somehow, when he hadn't been paying attention, he'd let himself fall in love with her.

Natalie rolled him over onto his back and kissed

his chest, ran her hands lovingly over his abdomen, seemingly determined to measure and memorize every ridge and bump. Her hair slithered over his belly and sides, making him quake with delicious sensation.

Without saying a word, she straddled him, the wet V of her hot sex gliding over the ridge of his arousal. She coated him in her juices, then arched up and slowly, carefully sank down, impaling herself on him.

Levi clenched his teeth so hard he feared they'd break, the pleasure was so intense. Her greedy muscles clamped around him as she slowly rocked back and forth, riding him. He watched her eyes flutter closed, her mouth curve into a wickedly sexual smile and her head roll languidly from side to side as she upped the tempo along with the music. His balls drew up so tight he could feel the climax building in the back of his dick, gathering force. He grasped her hips and then bent forward and drew the delicate bud of her breast into his mouth, suckling gently.

Natalie made a mewl of pleasure and her feminine muscles clasped tighter around him. She rode him harder, up and down, up and down, seemingly desperate for release to come.

"Oh, damn," she said, her voice a feminine growl. "You are— I want—"

Me, Levi thought. She wanted *him.* And he knew from her letters that she always had. The thought did it for him, tripped a trigger deep inside of him. The orgasm burst from his loins and he felt his body go rigid.

Her turn, Levi thought, then pressed his thumb against her swollen clit. Predictably she shattered. She spasmed hard around him, her feminine muscles milking the last of his release from his body. Breathing hard, she collapsed on top of him, her pebbled breasts against his chest, her tight little body still fisting around him as the last vestiges of her release ran through her.

Levi stroked his hands down her back, then traced the heart-shaped outline of her wonderful rump.

Lacking the courage to say "I love you," he mouthed the words against the top of her head and, for the first time in his life, wished he might have considered another path.

One that could have included her.

DETERMINED to keep from squalling until after she got home, Natalie curled up and settled contentedly against Levi's side. His fingers doodled pleasantly on her upper arm, bringing a smile to her lips.

She sighed and glanced around his room. "The Bat Cave," she said with dramatic emphasis. "At last."

Levi chuckled under his breath. "What?"

"Your room," she said. "I used to think of it as the Bat Cave. You usually kept your door closed. I could only get a peek when you came out of your room."

She felt his smile in the darkness. "And you *wanted* to?"

"Of course. This was your lair," she explained. "Your space. I wanted to know what it looked like. I thought it would be like taking a little peek at your soul. And, of course, I would have loved to pilfer through your stuff."

Levi laughed. "You're a nut."

"No I'm not." She jerked her head toward his Uncle Sam poster. "That's a look at who you are. And those trophies and that aftershave—and you know what impressed me the most?" she asked, propping up on her elbow to peer at him through the darkness.

"What?"

"Your bed was always made." She nodded succinctly. "You were tidy."

A hearty laugh rumbled up from his chest and he shot her a look that suggested she might have lost her mind. "I was tidy because I had to be. Dad would have tanned my hide if I hadn't made my bed."

"You mean you were tidy because you had to be, that at heart you were truly a slob?"

"I don't know if I'd go so far as to say I was a slob, but I sure as hell didn't make my bed because I wanted to."

She humphed, and lay back down. "Well, that's it, then, she said resignedly. "You are no longer officially perfect."

That wonderful chuckle she'd gotten so used to hearing near her ear sounded again. "Surely there's some way to redeem myself in your eyes," Levi said, trailing his fingers over the top of her hip.

"I don't know." She feigned concern. "I built a world of fantasies over this made bed."

His voice took on a husky timbre. "I've built a world of fantasies over you *in* my bed."

It had been the same for her, Natalie thought. "I got your letter today," she confessed. It was so strange to read letters from him while he was home, to read them and realize that, at the time he'd written to her, he still didn't know who she was.

"I figured as much. You know, since you snuck into my bed."

She smiled. "Hey, that was a cool fantasy. I'm glad that you gave me something to work with. I'd begun to worry that you didn't have any imagination at all."

He laughed. "No imagination?"

"You've got to be quiet," she said. "Your parents are going to hear us."

"Nah," Levi told her. "Once Dad turns on that

sound machine it's game over for them until it automatically goes off in the morning."

Slightly mollified, Natalie nodded. "It still makes me nervous."

"Not nervous enough to keep you from getting naked in my room and waiting for me." He gave her a squeeze. "That's the best damned thing that's ever happened in this room. Or in any room, for that matter. Thank you."

Warmth moved through her chest and settled like a blanket over her heart.

"I'm glad I could do something for you. You've been giving me my fantasies all week." She felt tears threaten again, but determinedly pushed them back. "You've been my dream come true, you know that?"

He grew quiet, then said, "It's been my pleasure."

Natalie looked at the digital bedside clock and sighed. She'd been here for hours. She really needed to go. "I guess I should crawl back out that window and head down to my place. You'll have to get up soon."

"Don't go yet," he said. "Stay with me a little while longer."

And before she could utter a single word of protest, he was kissing her again, then positioned himself between her thighs, filling her up, emptying her out, taking and giving and making her long for things that would never be.

Things like a life with him, morning coffee, walks on the beach, late-night dinners and making love. Like holidays and birthdays and little red-headed children with eyes the shade of toffee candy. Things like fighting and making up and sailing and holding hands.

Things like…life. With him.

Levi pushed into her over and over, almost desperately, as though he was trying to store her up for a rainy day, as though he genuinely cared for her the way she cared for him. He was urgent and reverent and relentless and she wanted desperately for him not to leave. For him to tell her that somehow they'd make it work.

But she knew that wouldn't happen. It couldn't. He was about to go halfway around the world to fight in a war that could, quite feasibly, take his life. He could walk out of her life tonight and never come back.

A sob rose in her throat, but she swallowed it, determined not to fall apart while he was here. He didn't want that. It wasn't fair. And her hero, her badass, her very heart, would feel terribly guilty because that's the man he was.

He was good, Natalie thought as release built up inside her once more. He was good and kind and wonderful and she absolutely loved him more than the air she was breathing.

"Look at me," he said. He threaded his fingers

through hers and lifted them over her head, stretching her out. She felt raw and open and exposed and...loved, God help her. "I want to watch you," he told her. "I want to see the look in your eyes when it happens."

Natalie arched against him, meeting him thrust for thrust, desperate for the same sort of connection. The same promise of something special. She wanted to see the look in his eyes when he let himself go, when he came into her.

He pushed, once, twice, a third time and then...

Bliss. Together.

They lay in the darkness for a few more minutes, then before she could change her mind or do something stupid, like beg him to change his life to accommodate her, Natalie quietly slipped from the bed and got dressed. She climbed back out through the window, then turned and propped her arms on the sill and rested her chin against them.

"I'm going to miss you," she said, though it wasn't enough, paled in comparison with the total devastation of her heart. *Breathe, Natalie. Just breathe.*

He traced her face with his gaze, then slid the pad of his thumb over her bottom lip. "I'm going to miss you, too."

"Thank you," she managed to say. "For everything. The past several days have been..." She sighed, searching for the right word. "Incredible."

He nodded. "The best damned leave I've ever had," he said. "You're wonderful, Nat."

"Be safe."

He smiled at her. "Always."

This was it, Natalie thought. Time to go. Time to leave. She managed another wobbly smile, then leaned forward and gave him a lingering kiss. "G'night."

She wouldn't say goodbye. Couldn't. It was too permanent. Too final.

She started to go.

"Hey, Nat," he called quietly.

She turned, hoping that he couldn't see the sheen of tears in her eyes. "Yeah?"

He gestured wordlessly, then managed a smile. *"Write."*

A broken laugh came apart in her throat and the tears she'd been stemming for hours suddenly slipped past her lashes. "I will," she promised.

13

Dear Levi,
I don't know quite how to say this, but I've
decided that I'm going to have to hate you.
Loving you is too hard. I know that may sound
irrational, but…it is what it is…

"YOU READY to go, Dad?" Natalie asked, filling her
water bottle from her father's kitchen faucet. Though
her heart wasn't exactly into combing at the moment,
Natalie nevertheless couldn't bring herself to skip a
day. That perfect piece she might miss haunted her,
even when her heart was broken.

"I think I'll pass this morning, hon. I've got some
things to do around here."

Stunned, Natalie stood glued to the spot. *Pass?* He
hadn't *passed* in five years, not a day since her
mother had died. "O-okay," she said, because she
couldn't manage anything else.

Sitting placidly at the kitchen table, as though he

hadn't just dropped a bomb onto her already shattered world, her father rattled his paper. "I did a bit of thinking while I was at your uncle Milton's house and I realized that I've been smothering you."

"No, Dad, you—"

He dropped the paper and his sad eyes met hers. "Yes I have. I know it. Have known it." He swallowed. "After I lost your mother I was so angry at the sea, so fearful of what it could take from me. I even considered selling this house and moving away."

This was definitely the morning for shocks, Natalie thought, as his comment bolted through her. "You did?"

He nodded. "Do you know why I didn't?"

"No," she said, swallowing, because it was a lie. He'd stayed for her. Because Bethel Bay was her home.

"Because you love it here, Natalie, and I couldn't bear to be away from you. The ocean and your art—" He shrugged helplessly. "—it's who you are. So I knew that I couldn't leave because that would mean leaving you. That's when I decided that if I couldn't move away, then I could at least keep you safe. It didn't matter that you were a strong swimmer. Like your mother," he added. "Or that you rarely ventured into more than a foot of water when we're combing." He smiled, though the grin was anything but amused. It was so sad it made her chest ache. "Nothing mattered but making sure you were okay." He sighed heavily. "It became my mission, you see. I *had* to protect you. Because if I was focusing on protecting you, then I wouldn't have to face my own life, deal with my own loss. Your mother and me, we were supposed to grow old together. We were supposed to take RV trips and spoil grandchildren. I was robbed, you see, and I didn't want to face it."

Her throat tightened. She joined him at the table and took his hand in hers. "Oh, Dad."

"I know that you're hurting right now, Natalie, and you miss your man. But you haven't lost him, honey," he said, in a weary voice that held a wealth of meaning. "You've only lost if you give up. Don't give up, honey. Love, when it's real, is worth it."

She didn't doubt him, Natalie thought. She just didn't know how to make it work.

"How ARE things going over there?" Adam asked two weeks later, when Levi managed to get a call out to home.

"The same as they were when I left," Levi said. "One step forward, two steps back. Two steps forward, one step back."

"Yeah, well, so long as you stay a step ahead, that's all I care about," Adam said. "How are the guys?"

"Fine. Wondering when you're going to be back in business. Forrester says hi, by the way, and he's glad to hear that you're losing weight."

"Hey, shut the hell up," Adam said, laughing. "I'll

have you know I've been hitting the gym every damned day."

"That's good news, little brother."

"Damned Winnie. I still can't believe she said that to me."

Though it officially sounded like a complaint, Levi could tell his brother was secretly pleased with Winnie's candor.

"That's the hell of it when it comes to women," Levi said, staring at a picture of Natalie that he'd stolen from Adam. "You never know what they're going to say."

Adam sighed. "You miss her, don't you?"

He could ask who, but what was the point? Levi passed a hand over his face. "Yeah," he admitted. "More than I could have imagined."

And he meant that.

Honestly, he didn't have any idea how these other guys did it. How they walked away from their families—wives and children—to do this job. He had a whole new appreciation for the guys who were here with loved ones back home. The ones who carried pictures of their children in their pockets and kept snapshots of their wives over their beds.

He got it now. Truly, genuinely *got it.*

"Well, if it makes you feel any better, she's a wreck."

Levi straightened, alarm knifing through him. "Why the hell would that make me feel better?"

"Because misery loves company, I guess." Adam sighed heavily. "Of course, I warned you about this, so I hope you know that I'm going to kick your ass with my brand-new shiny leg when you get home."

Though he should have been more interested in the fact that his brother wanted to kill him, he was too distracted by the other part of the sentence to care. "You got it?"

"It's awesome. Seriously. I can hurt you with it. I'm going to knock your nuts up between your shoulder blades."

Though he knew Adam was just yanking his chain, there was a hint of truthfulness in the threat. Which only served to make him feel worse. He and Natalie were adults. They'd known how things would play out. But...

"She's that bad, is she?"

"She's putting on a brave face," Adam said. "She's still coming down and playing cards and I've been going combing with her the past few mornings. But there's a sadness around her eyes that wasn't there before and she's not sleeping."

"How do you know that?"

"Because I know her, dammit," he said, exasperated. "She's been staying up—working, if I had my guess."

Levi's chest ached and let go a sigh. "I'd fix it if I could, Adam. But I don't know how."

"Yeah, well, you're going to have to figure it out,"

Adam said, as though a plausible solution was just a good thinking session away, as if he could just drag a remedy from thin air. "I can't stand to see her this way. And I sure as hell can't fix it. Because I'm not you." He paused. "I know phone time is hard to come by, but you'd better be writing her."

"I am," Levi said. He'd written her every day since he'd left. Hell, he'd written the first letter while on the plane back over. He couldn't stop thinking about her either. He woke up and he wondered what she was doing, he went to bed and he wished she was there beside him. And the things that happened in his dreams…they weren't nearly as wonderful as the real thing.

In short, he was a wreck, and if didn't get a grip he was going to screw up and the outcome wouldn't be pretty.

As if reading his mind, Adam issued a warning. "For the time being, you just keep your head out of your ass and focus on what you're doing. You can figure the Natalie thing out when your tour's over."

"Adam, there's nothing to figure out. She's in Bethel Bay. Her career, her family, her life is in Bethel Bay. Mine's here. I've been over it six ways to Sunday and this story just isn't going to have a happy ending."

"Bullshit. You're writing the ending. Make it happen."

Levi felt his patience snap. "How? How am I supposed to do that? If I ask her to come with me, then I'm taking her away from what she loves."

"I think you're underestimating just how in love with you she is."

"Now," Levi argued. "But what about later? What about when she's missing the beach and her father and all her friends and family? What about when I'm deployed and I'm not there for her?" He sighed heavily. "I've been over it. I've thought about it. It's a no-win situation."

"You'd never consider coming out? Getting a different job?"

"It's not just a *job,* Adam. It's who I am. Hell, you of all people ought to know that."

Adam's silence echoed over the line. "You're right. Shitty suggestion. I'm sorry. You know, bro, I just want you both to be happy. And I know that you're happy together."

He knew it, too. But knowing it and making it happen were two completely different things.

"She could always come back to Bethel Bay when you were deployed," Adam suggested. "Would it be a conventional relationship? No. But it's better than what you've got. Which is nothing."

Feeling like he'd totally screwed things up, Levi leaned against the wall and considered what his brother had just said.

"Let me ask you something, Levi. No bullshit here, okay? Truth time. Gut-check, you understand?"

Levi rubbed the bridge of his nose. "Yeah."

"Do you love her? I don't mean do you like her a lot or are you infatuated or do you want to have lots of sex with her. I mean, do you *love* her?"

He didn't even have to think about it, Levi realized. "I do."

Adam's breath echoed over the line. "Then you'll figure it out."

His brother certainly had a lot more faith in him than he did, Levi thought. Because he didn't know what in the hell to do.

NATALIE SAT cross-legged on her couch, a wad of tissue in her hand and little tissue balls lying all around her. An empty cookie container and soda cans littered her coffee table.

Winnie stood just inside her front door, mouth hanging open, a lavender box of what smelled like petits fours in her hands.

"What the hell are you doing?"

Natalie gestured wearily toward the TV and new tears filled her eyes. "I love this movie," she said. "It has everything. Have you ever noticed that? It's not just romantic love, but *all* kinds of love. New love, old love, love between friends, love between families, betrayed love, unrequited love." She sniffed loudly. "It's a wonderful, wonderful example of life."

Winnie looked genuinely concerned. "It's called *Love, Actually*. What did you think it was going to be about?"

"This is my favorite scene," Natalie told her, aiming the remote control at the television. "Do you see what he's doing? How he's telling her that he loves her with those poster boards? How he can move on? Isn't that r-romantic? Isn't it wonderful?"

Winnie batted a couple of tissue balls aside, then sat down, opened the pastry box and handed her a petit four. "Is this supposed to be symbolic of you learning to go on without Levi? Because I've got to be honest. You're starting to make me sick."

Natalie almost choked. "What? Sick?"

"Yes, sick. Honestly, Natalie, you knew that this thing between you was never going to be more than it was. You knew that he'd go back to Iraq, that he was just as firmly invested in his career as you are in yours. What did you think was going to happen when he left? Did you think you'd be the same? That things would just go back to normal?"

Natalie blinked. "I thought it would be better. I thought I would be happier." She gestured toward her friend. "I took your friggin' advice, didn't I? If it was wrong, then why the hell did you give it to me?"

"I didn't say it was wrong. I just said it's time to

accept things the way they are. Be happy for the time you had together. Be happy for the relationship that you had. It's a damn sight better than the one on paper you started with."

Be that as it may, it wasn't enough. She wanted him. *Needed* him in her life. Natalie slumped back against her couch. "I know that! You think I don't know that?" She felt her bottom lip shake. "What I didn't know was that it would be this hard. That I would miss him this terribly. I feel like a part of me is missing, a part that I'm not altogether certain I'm ever going to get back. I feel broken and I'm miserable and I'm lonely. I'm sorry if I'm not 'bouncing back' the way you think I should, but I can't help it. And for the time being, I *like* feeling this way. It makes me happy."

Winnie gaped at her. "Let me make sure I understand this correctly. You're happy being miserable?"

"Yes. It's how I'm supposed to feel right now." She gestured to the self-help book on her end table. "According to everything I've read, this is how I'm supposed to feel at this stage and that makes me happy. Because, clearly, I'm *normal*."

Winnie snatched the book off the table and stalked to the trash can, where she determinedly threw it. "You've lost your freaking mind, you know that?" She jerked her head toward the bedroom. "Go get dressed. We're going to do something."

Natalie looked at her suspiciously. "To do what?"

"Doesn't matter. Anything is better than watching you sit here and fester in a pool of your own snot and tears." She grabbed her hands and yanked Natalie from the couch. "Come on. Move." She sniffed delicately. "And bathe."

Ten minutes later, feeling marginally cleaner if not better, Natalie walked out of her bedroom. Winnie had tidied the living room and had stolen her copy of *Love, Actually.* She could see the DVD case poking out of the top of her friend's purse.

Winnie looked her over and nodded approvingly. "Better," she said. "You still look like you've had an allergic reaction of some sort—"

"That would be to heartbreak," Natalie said. "I'm allergic to having my heart broken."

"—but you'll do."

Do for what? But Winnie was right. She needed to get out of her house. She'd been holed up here since Levi had left, alternately squalling, puking, watching romantic comedies and working on the stag.

She'd finished the piece, actually, and for some reason she'd had it in her head that completing the stag would give her some sort of insight, some sort of closure. That being done with the project would change her on the inside.

It hadn't.

She was still broken.

Though she was still working a bit on the doe, she'd moved the stag into her bedroom and placed it where it was the first thing she saw every morning when she woke up and the last thing she saw before going to sleep. In between, sometimes she'd dream of Levi and sometimes she wouldn't, but she always awoke with the same lonely feeling in her chest, the same sad realization that, despite the fact that she'd known the rules going in, she was hopelessly, miserably in love with a man she couldn't have.

It was horrendously unfair.

Winnie peered into her room and saw the stag. She let go a little sigh and her gaze softened. "It's beautiful, Nat."

Natalie swallowed thickly. It was, she knew. Some of her very best work. "Thank you."

"Have you finished the doe?"

"Still working on her."

Winnie made a low noise in her throat, as though there was some sort of hidden meaning there, but Natalie didn't have the strength to pursue it. She blew out a breath, put out fresh water for Geraldine and looked at her friend. "So where are we going?"

"You'll see when we get there."

Whatever, Natalie thought.

"I think I saw your dad's truck parked over at Eloise Dawson's house on the way here," Winnie remarked.

Despite her own misery, Natalie chuckled. "I'm sure you did. I'm relatively certain that he's been spending the night over there."

Winnie chuckled. "Sounds like that trip to Uncle Milton's stirred some things up for your father."

It sure as hell had, Natalie thought. She didn't know exactly what had transpired, but it had been good for both of them. Her father had returned with a spring in his step and a new kind of aftershave and, most shocking of all, no longer insisted on going combing with her. That conversation had been an eye-opener, but she was so very thankful for the progress.

Oh, and he'd sold the lot next door.

It absolutely blew her mind, what little of it was not preoccupied with Levi.

At any rate, other than being a wretched lump of human flesh pining away for her soldier, she had to admit things were looking up around Camp Rowland. As for the lot, when she'd asked who he'd sold it to, all her father had said was that she didn't need to worry, that he was keeping it in the family. More than likely one of her cousins had finally worn him down, Natalie had concluded, and in the grand scheme of things, she just didn't care. She was too busy trying to remember to breathe in and out all day.

Winnie drove a short distance down the road and surprised Natalie by pulling into the McPherson driveway. "We're here," she announced as she shifted into Park.

"What?" Natalie frowned and looked at her friend. "What are we doing here?"

"Adam asked me to bring you by."

For reasons she couldn't explain, Natalie felt betrayed. "You're talking to him that much, are you?"

A shadow moved over Winnie's face, making Natalie instantly regret the petty question. "No," she said. "But he did come round the bakery this morning and told me that he had something to show you. He said he'd called several times, but couldn't get you to answer the phone."

She hadn't been answering the phone for anybody. She didn't want to talk about how awful and wretched she felt. It only served to make her more pathetic.

"Sorry," Natalie mumbled. "I thought the two of you were making some progress."

Winnie smiled sadly. "I did, too."

"Oh, Winnie. I'm such a self-absorbed friend."

Winnie gave her head a sanctimonious nod. "I forgive you. Now let's go."

Winnie led the way around to the back of the house and they found Adam in the screened-in porch, reading a true-crime paperback.

"I didn't know you read," Natalie said, more than a little surprised at his new pastime.

Adam feigned outrage and jerked his head toward the boat. "I do. And I can write, too. It's some of that fancy learnin' I picked up in school."

Natalie looked out at the dock and Levi's boat. She inhaled sharply when she saw the new name that had been stenciled onto the back.

Second Helping.

Adam grinned. "Levi told me that it would have a significant meaning for you."

New tears pricked her lids. "It does."

"He wanted me to show it to you."

She turned and shot him a grateful look over her shoulder. "Thank you."

He quirked a brow. "Want to share the inside joke?"

Natalie managed a watery grin. "Nope. Just use your imagination."

And, dammit, she was going to have to use hers to figure out a way to make this work. They had to. The alternative wasn't working for her at all. When Levi came home, Natalie promised herself, she'd have some sort of plan in place. Anything was better than this. Any arrangement was better than not having one at all, right?

14

Dear Levi,
I saw the boat today. Love the new name.
Would it be tacky of me to ask for a third
helping? Fourth even? Though I've tried to
"diet" I still find myself very hungry…

Six weeks later…

LEVI DROPPED his duffel bag on Natalie's front porch
and prepared to ring her doorbell. It had been two
months since he'd last seen her, though he'd gotten
dozens of letters from her during that time. Letters
that had made him laugh, made him smile, made
him miss her all the more. Letters that had made
him hard, letters that had enflamed him.

Despite the fact that he'd told himself that things
wouldn't work between them, that they were each
too invested in their own lives, Levi couldn't let it go.
Couldn't stop thinking about what his brother had

told him. That a nontraditional relationship would be better than nothing at all.

Initially, he'd rejected the idea out of hand. How could he ask her to live like that? To do things so very differently from their own parents? To live apart for long stretches of time, but still be essentially... together?

Then again, how could he not?

Because doing it the way they'd been doing it for the past two months had just about killed him. He could not—and didn't want to—live without her.

Natalie Rowland filled a void in his life that Levi had never been aware existed...until she wasn't there anymore. She completed him. Made him more. Made him want to be better.

More than anything, though, he just wanted to be with her. Whenever he could. Period. And as Adam had so insightfully pointed out, that was better than the nothing they had now.

So no, this definitely wasn't going to be a conventional relationship—they each had things that were too important to simply give up—but they could make it work. Or at least, he wanted to try.

And there was one fantasy of hers that he'd never fulfilled, one of the very first she'd ever written to him. He'd committed it to memory, because he wanted to get it just right.

Dear Levi,
I dreamed about you again last night. I dreamed you were home and, more importantly, mine. I dreamed you wanted me, *really* wanted me, that you walked through my front door, our eyes locked, and a second later you were on me, taking me hard and fast against the door. You kissed me as though you needed my breath to breathe, you took my breasts into your mouth and suckled the peaks until I almost came. You slipped your wickedly talented fingers into my panties and I rubbed myself against you, satisfied…but not. Wanting more. Needing more. I'm hot and muddled now, remembering.

That made two of them, Levi thought as he finally summoned the courage to ring her doorbell.

He heard her approach, knew the exact instant her eye went to the peephole and discerned who was there.

She opened the door, her face a mask of shock and hope and joy.

Levi's gaze locked with hers. He showed her everything he had—the frustration, the longing, the desire, the love. Bared it all, and knew when she recognized it because she gave a soft little gasp.

He strode inside, purposely shut her door, then whirled her around and backed her up against it.

Then he kissed her.

Hard and deep, long and slow, he tangled his tongue around hers, giving her everything he had. Sweet Lord, how he loved her. She tasted so damned wonderful.

She came alive in his arms, feeding at his mouth, running her hands through his hair. She kneaded his shoulders and rubbed herself against him, just as mindless, just as desperate as he was.

Levi freed himself from his pants, lifted her up and pushed her sundress out of the way, then nudged her panties aside. A moment later he was in heaven. He was in her. And he could breathe again.

"I need you," he said, pushing in and out of her, flexing his hips as she welcomed him deep inside her hot little body. "We have to figure out a way to make this work."

Natalie whimpered against him, tightened her greedy feminine muscles around his shaft. "I agree. But could we finish this first? Because—" she gasped, "I want— I need—"

"Me," he finished for her, pistoning in and out of her. "You need *me*. You want *me*."

With a long slow howl, he levered in and out, frantically racing for release, for the absolute pleasure he'd only find with her. Her breath came in broken little puffs and he could feel her nearing climax, could feel it gathering in his own loins.

A cry suddenly tore from her throat and she

spasmed hard around him, an insistent grip and release that triggered his own release. He bucked hard and angled up, planting his feet firmly beneath them to keep from falling down as the orgasm washed through him, threatening to buckle his knees. He went weak, God help him, almost dizzy. With effort, he pulled away from her and righted her dress.

Natalie kissed him tenderly, reverently, and her brown eyes glittered with unshed tears. "I thought we'd already established that I wanted you," she said, her voice thick.

Levi brushed a kiss over her temple and sighed heavily. "The thing is…what we haven't fully established is that I'm in love with you."

Her eyes widened and she seemed to melt against him. "You're right. I don't think we've established that."

He pretended to think about it. "Right. Well, I'm here to correct that." He cupped her jaw. "I'm in love with you, Nat, and I know the logistics are going to be a nightmare, but I was sort of hoping that a.) you loved me, too, and b.) you'd want to try and make this work."

A cautious smile faltered over her lips. "Make it work how?"

He shook his head. "First things first. Do you love me?"

She framed his face with her hands, the gesture

so simple and heartfelt that a nebulous obstruction gathered in his throat. "You must not have gotten my latest letter."

He drew back and looked at her. "Oh?"

"Yes, because if you had, you would know beyond a shadow of a doubt that I do love you. With every fiber in my being."

He rested his forehead against hers. "I like every fiber in your being."

She grinned softly. "You still didn't answer my question."

"What question was that?"

"How are we going to make it work? I'm here, you're—" She gestured helplessly. "—wherever you are next."

"Germany."

Her eyes widened. "Germany? Really. Er…"

"Here's what I was thinking," Levi said. "I was thinking that you could marry me and we would split time between here and, in the immediate future, Germany."

"Split time?"

He squeezed her for emphasis. "We can make it work, Nat. I know that it won't be an ordinary arrangement, but I can't stand the idea of the alternative." His gaze searched hers. "I love you. I want to be with you. The rest—" He shrugged. "—it doesn't matter. All that matters is that you're mine."

"You would be happy living like that?"

"I'll be happy with *you*," he said. "We can have both, you see? It doesn't have be either-or. We can have it all. My question is, can you live that way? Would you even want to?"

Her coffee-colored eyes searched his, consideringly. "I'd have to be home in the summer. It's the high season and—"

He nodded succinctly. "Done. Home in the summer, whether I can come or not. But winter with me?" he asked cautiously, a hopeful element in his voice he refused to hide.

She smiled, and happiness infused her wonderfully familiar face. "Of course. I'll need you to keep me warm."

"You never answered *my* question," he reminded her.

A line emerged between her delicate brows. "What question?"

"Will you marry me?"

"Oh, Lord, yes," she said, as though it were a foregone conclusion.

His chest expanded almost painfully and the smile that slid over his lips had to make him look like an utter fool. But he was *her* fool. He glanced around her living room. "We're going to need a bigger place."

"We are? For what?"

"For all the children we're going to have."

She laughed delightedly. "We'll have to build up, then, because I'm out of room on this lot."

Levi chewed the inside of his cheek. "No you're not."

She drew back and gave him a suspicious look. "What?"

"I talked John into selling *me* the lot next door." He looked up and pretended to think about it. "Actually, I called to talk to him about buying it, but when I asked him for your hand, he gave it to us as a wedding gift."

There was that melting look again. "You asked my dad for my hand?"

"I did."

Natalie kissed him again. "You really are a hero, you know that?"

He shrugged. "Hero, second helping…doesn't matter so long as I'm yours."

Natalie threaded her fingers through his and gently tugged him toward her bedroom. "You definitely are. And I'm hungry."

Though he didn't believe he could be distracted from her, Levi's gaze landed on the stag. "You moved him into your room?"

She smiled again, just the faintest quirk of her lips. "I did. I wanted you in here with me."

"Me?" Levi asked, staring at the beautiful, hauntingly familiar work of art.

"Yes, you. He's my interpretation of you."

Touched beyond words, Levi looked down at her. "Natalie, I don't know what to say. It's… It's remarkable. I'm honored. Thank you." He frowned as a thought struck. "Where's the doe?"

"She's still in the studio. I'm not done with her yet."

Oh, no, Levi thought. That wouldn't do. He went to get her, then brought her back into the bedroom and carefully deposited her next to the stag. "You can't separate them," Levi told her. "It makes them miserable."

Natalie considered the two pieces side by side. "You know what? I was wrong. She is complete… now that she's with you."

"I love you."

She smiled at him. "So you've said."

Levi picked her up and tossed her on the bed, then followed her down. "Some things bear repeating."

"Like second helpings?"

He nuzzled her neck. "Definitely second helpings."

Epilogue

One week later...

Dear Adam,

Just wanted to pen a quick note to let you know that we're having a wonderful time. Levi was right. The pyramids are *amazing*. We've toured several tombs and taken a camel ride through the Valley of the Kings. Pretty damned fearless, your brother. Naturally, I find that infinitely appealing. Of course, I find virtually everything appealing about my new husband, so that shouldn't come as any surprise.

Though I wasn't sure I would enjoy this travel thing, I have to admit I'm having the time of my life. I like breathing different air, too—or at least the same air that your brother is breathing. (Though naturally I miss Bethel Bay.)

Hope things are going well with you, that you're getting stronger every day. I'll write

from Greece. I'm looking forward to wading the shores of the Mediterranean. Who knows what sort of treasure I'll find, though admittedly I've already found the greatest one—love. And now that I've officially sickened you with my happiness, I'll sign off.
Hugs and love,
Natalie

P.S. Stop avoiding Winnie, you stubborn ass. She's good for you.

* * * * *

*Celebrate 60 years of pure reading
pleasure with Harlequin®!*

*Harlequin Presents® is proud to introduce its
gripping new miniseries,*
THE ROYAL HOUSE OF KAREDES.
*An exquisite coronation diamond, split as a
symbol of a warring royal family's feud, is
missing! But whoever reunites the
diamond halves will rule all….*

*Welcome to eight brand-new titles that unfold to
reveal the stories of kings and queens, princes and
princesses torn apart by pride and power, but
finally reunited by love.*

*Step into the world of Karedes with
BILLIONAIRE PRINCE, PREGNANT MISTRESS.
Available July 2009 from Harlequin Presents®.*

Alexandros Karedes, snow dusting the shoulders of his leather jacket and glittering like jewels in his dark hair, stood at the door. Maria felt the blood drain from her head.

"Good evening, Ms. Santos."

His voice was as she remembered it. Deep. Husky. Perfect English, but with the faintest hint of a Greek accent. And cold, as cold as it had been that awful morning she would never forget, when he'd accused her of horrible things, called her terrible names....

"Aren't you going to ask me in?"

She fought for composure. Last time they'd faced each other, they'd been on his turf. Now they were on hers. She was in command here, and that meant everything.

"There's a sign on the door downstairs," she said, her tone every bit as frigid as his. "It says, 'No soliciting or vagrants.'"

His lips drew back in a wolfish grin. "Very amusing."

"What do you want, Prince Alexandros?"

A tight smile eased across his mouth and it killed her that even now, knowing he was a vicious, arrogant man, she couldn't help but notice what a handsome mouth it was. Chiseled. Generous. Beautiful, like the rest of him, which made him living proof that beauty could, indeed, be only skin deep.

"Such formality, Maria. You were hardly so proper the last time we were together."

She knew his choice of words was deliberate. She felt her face heat; she couldn't help that but she damned well didn't have to let him lure her into a verbal sparring match.

"I'll ask you once more, your highness. What do you want?"

"Ask me in and I'll tell you."

"I have no intention of asking you in. Tell me why you're here or don't. It's your choice, just as it will be my choice to shut the door in your face."

He laughed. It infuriated her but she could hardly blame him. He was tall—six two, six three—and though he stood with one shoulder leaning against the door frame, hands tucked casually into the pockets of his jacket, his pose was deceptive. He was strong, with the leanly muscled body of a well-trained athlete.

She remembered his body with painful clarity. The feel of him under her hands. The power of him moving over her. The taste of him on her tongue.

Suddenly, he straightened, his laughter gone. "I have not come this distance to stand in your doorway," he said coldly, "and I am not going to leave until I am ready to do so. I suggest you stand aside and stop behaving like a petulant child."

A petulant child? Was that what he thought? This man who had spent hours making love to her and had then accused her of—of trading her body for profit?

Except it had not been love, it had been sex. And the sooner she got rid of him, the better.

She let go of the doorknob and stepped aside. "You have five minutes."

He strolled past her, bringing cold air and the scent of the night with him. She swung toward him, arms folded. He reached past her, pushed the door closed, then folded his arms, too. She wanted to open the door again but she'd be damned if she was going to get into a who's-in-charge-here argument with him. She was in charge, and he would surely see a tussle over the ground rules as a sign of weakness.

Instead, she looked past him at the big clock above her worktable.

"Ten seconds gone," she said briskly. "You're wasting time, your highness."

"What I have to say will take longer than five minutes."

"Then you'll just have to learn to economize. More than five minutes, I'll call the police."

Instantly, his hand was wrapped around her wrist. He tugged her toward him, his dark-chocolate eyes almost black with anger.

"You do that and I'll tell every tabloid shark I can contact about how Maria Santos tried to buy a five-hundred-thousand-dollar commission by seducing a prince." He smiled thinly. "They'll lap it up."

* * * * *

*What will it take for this
billionaire prince to realize
he's falling in love with his mistress…?*
Look for
*BILLIONAIRE PRINCE,
PREGNANT MISTRESS*
by Sandra Marton.
Available July 2009 from Harlequin Presents®.

We'll be spotlighting a different series every month throughout 2009 to celebrate our 60th anniversary.

Look for Harlequin® Presents in July!

TWO CROWNS, TWO ISLANDS, ONE LEGACY

A royal family, torn apart by pride and its lust for power, reunited by purity and passion

Step into the world of Karedes
beginning this July with

BILLIONAIRE PRINCE, PREGNANT MISTRESS
by
Sandra Marton

Eight volumes to collect and treasure!

HARLEQUIN® *Blaze*™

Heat up those summer months
with a double dose of HOT!

Hot men, that is.

Look for Blaze's upcoming miniseries:

American Heroes:
The Texas Rangers

Real men, real heroes!

Check out:

Hard to Resist

by SAMANTHA HUNTER
July 2009

and

One Good Man

by ALISON KENT
September 2009

Available wherever Harlequin books are sold.

---

red-hot reads

REQUEST YOUR FREE BOOKS!

2 FREE NOVELS PLUS 2 FREE GIFTS!

HARLEQUIN®

Blaze™

Red-hot reads!

YES! Please send me 2 FREE Harlequin® Blaze™ novels and my 2 FREE gifts (gifts are worth about $10). After receiving them, if I don't wish to receive any more books, I can return the shipping statement marked "cancel". If I don't cancel, I will receive 6 brand-new novels every month and be billed just $4.24 per book in the U.S. or $4.71 per book in Canada. That's a savings of 15% off the cover price. It's quite a bargain. Shipping and handling is just 50¢ per book.* I understand that accepting the 2 free books and gifts places me under no obligation to buy anything. I can always return a shipment and cancel at any time. Even if I never buy another book, the two free books and gifts are mine to keep forever.

151 HDN EYS2 351 HDN EYTE

Name	(PLEASE PRINT)	
Address		Apt. #
City	State/Prov.	Zip/Postal Code

Signature (if under 18, a parent or guardian must sign)

Mail to the **Harlequin Reader Service:**
IN U.S.A.: P.O. Box 1867, Buffalo, NY 14240-1867
IN CANADA: P.O. Box 609, Fort Erie, Ontario L2A 5X3

Not valid to current subscribers of Harlequin Blaze books.

Want to try two free books from another line?
Call 1-800-873-8635 or visit www.morefreebooks.com.

* Terms and prices subject to change without notice. Prices do not include applicable taxes. N.Y. residents add applicable sales tax. Canadian residents will be charged applicable provincial taxes and GST. Offer not valid in Quebec. This offer is limited to one order per household. All orders subject to approval. Credit or debit balances in a customer's account(s) may be offset by any other outstanding balance owed by or to the customer. Please allow 4 to 6 weeks for delivery. Offer available while quantities last.

Your Privacy: Harlequin Books is committed to protecting your privacy. Our Privacy Policy is available online at www.eHarlequin.com or upon request from the Reader Service. From time to time we make our lists of customers available to reputable third parties who may have a product or service of interest to you. If you would prefer we not share your name and address, please check here. ☐

HB09R3

In 2009 Harlequin celebrates
60 years of pure reading pleasure!

We're marking this occasion by offering
16 **FREE** full books to download and read.

We invite you to visit and share the Web site
with your friends, family
and anyone who enjoys reading.

HARLEQUIN *Blaze*

COMING NEXT MONTH
Available June 30, 2009

#477 ENDLESS SUMMER Julie Kenner, Karen Anders, Jill Monroe
Three surfer chicks + three hot guys = one endless summer. The Maui beaches will never be the same after these couples hit the waves and live their sexiest dreams to the fullest!

#478 HARD TO RESIST Samantha Hunter
American Heroes
Sexy, straight-as-an-arrow Texas Ranger Jarod Wyatt is awestruck by the New York skyline and the stunning photographer snapping his portrait. As soon as Lacey Graham spies the hunk through her lens she knows she has to have him…even if she has to commit a crime to get the good cop's attention!

#479 MAKE ME YOURS Betina Krahn
Blaze Historicals
Mariah Eller was only trying to save her inn from being trashed. So how did she manage to attract the unwanted—and erotic—attention of the Prince of Wales? Not that being desired by royalty is bad—except Mariah much prefers Jack St. Lawrence, the prince's sexy best friend....

#480 TWIN SEDUCTION Cara Summers
The Wrong Bed: Again and Again
Jordan Ware is in over her head. According to her late mother's will, she has to trade places with a twin sister she didn't know she had. She thinks it will be tricky, but possible…until she finds herself in bed with her twin's fiancé.

#481 THE SOLDIER Rhonda Nelson
Uniformly Hot!
Army Ranger Adam McPherson is back home, thanks to a roadside bomb that cost him part of his leg. But he's not out yet. He's been offered a position in the Special Forces once he's back on his feet. The problem? His childhood nemesis seems determined to keep him off his feet—and in her bed.…

#482 THE MIGHTY QUINNS: TEAGUE Kate Hoffmann
Quinns Down Under
Romeo and Juliet, Outback-style. Teague Quinn has loved Haley Fraser since they were both kids. But time and feuding families got in the way. Now Teague and Haley are both back home—and back in bed! Can they make first love last the second time around?

www.eHarlequin.com